Davis snorted. "Yeah, well, the little peacemaker tried to get rid of me when I didn't kowtow to Aaron and the advisor. I don't think she fully realizes the precarious position she and her clan are in right now."

"On the contrary, I am quite aware, which is why I don't see the need to make the matter worse by antagonizing everyone around me."

Davis slowly swiveled his head to meet Bethany's glare. She stood in the open doorway to the bathroom with her arms wrapped tightly around her waist. Her dark gaze pinned on him. She'd changed into a blue dress. It accentuated her tiny waist, skimming just below her knees, allowing him an appreciative view of her trim legs. Her pursed lips only accentuated the pink little bow of her mouth. He couldn't help but imagine what it might be like to grab a taste.

An amused chuckle sounded in his ear. "She doesn't sound very happy with you, Davis. Are you sure you want to stay?"

"Yeah, I'm sure."

Scent of Betrayal

by

Denise Carbo

Shifters of Rishard, Book Two

Scent of Betrayal

Cover Art by *Rae Monet, Inc. Design*

The Wild Rose Press, Inc.
PO Box 708
Adams Basin, NY 14410-0708
Visit us at www.thewildrosepress.com

Publishing History
First Fantasy Rose Edition, 2019
Print ISBN 978-1-5092-2710-5
Digital ISBN 978-1-5092-2711-2

Shifters of Rishard, Book Two
Published in the United States of America

Dedication

To my mother-in-law,
without a doubt my number one fan.
Thank you for all your support and excitement
over my books.
It means the world to me.

Chapter One

The cool spring air blew across his snout as he ran through the woods, erasing all traces of the tantalizing scent which had both intrigued and enraged him over the past several weeks. The heavy aroma of pine and earth from his beloved Wyoming mountains filled his nostrils. Muscles bunched and extended as he leaped over a fallen tree and continued his trek. Towering evergreens and rocky terrain blurred at the edges of his vision when he increased his speed. It could be his last chance to run in his wolf form for a while.

The pads of his paws made light thumps against the pine needle laden ground. His previous soft pants increased, creating tiny clouds of breath in the chilly air, and he slowed his speed. His ears twitched toward the sound of water cascading over rocks, and he loped off in that direction. A narrow stream meandered down the mountain. He looked around the area before dipping his head to the small pool and taking a sip—the icy water trickled down his throat.

Leaping onto an enormous boulder with a flat top on the bank of the stream, he sat on his haunches. A spider web spanned the distance between two branches directly overhead. Morning dew glistened as the rising sun shone on the web's incandescent threads. Thick carpets of green moss covered the crevices of the rocks dotting the stream's path. An owl hooted farther up the mountain, and he swiveled his head in its direction. An answering call echoed back before they both went silent.

Raising his nose, he scented the wind and angled his head toward the stream below him. Light footsteps meandered his way along the stream's edge. The familiar scent held him in place, for he recognized who approached.

Curiosity rose within him.

Greer ambled into view. His black jeans and shirt blended in with the dark shadows beneath the trees, where the sunlight hadn't yet reached. Easily scaling the rocks, he climbed up and sat down a few feet away—quietly staring up at the lightening sky through the treetops.

They sat in companionable silence for several moments. He glanced at Greer, knowing his friend could sit there all day without saying a word. Blowing out a rough breath, he stood on all fours. A brief shudder rippled over his form. Davis shifted back to his human body and dropped down to sit on the rock, wincing at the cold, rough texture against his skin.

"Well? What brings you out here?"

Greer snagged a piece of broken branch and examined the six-inch piece of knotty wood. "Why did you volunteer to escort Leitner's sister back to the Euro clan?"

Davis shrugged. "Why not? I'm curious to see what's happening over there now that the leadership of the clan is up for grabs. Should be entertaining at the very least, and maybe informative. I think it's best to keep an eye on what the other clans are up to, especially after Donald's murder, don't you?"

"You think someone besides Bryant Leitner had a hand in Donald's murder?"

"I know he did the deed, but his journal left some questions. Maybe he was bat shit crazy and acted alone, but what if he wasn't? What if someone else was working with him? I want everyone responsible."

Greer painstakingly stripped the bark off the broken branch, revealing the lighter toned wood lying beneath. "If he didn't act alone, the person may have gone into hiding." He glanced at Davis. "Or the person is one of those battling for power over the clan and will want to eliminate anyone who might get in his or her way."

Davis placed a hand over his heart. "You worried about me Greer? I didn't think you cared."

The expression on Greer's face didn't change. "You're part of my clan, just making sure you understand what you might be heading into." His attention returned to the wood in his hands. "What about the woman?"

"What woman? Bethany? What about her?" Davis shifted position. Sitting on a rock as a wolf was one thing, sitting bare-ass naked on one as a man was entirely different, and uncomfortable.

"She's part of the ruling family of the Euro clan."

"You don't still think she had anything to do with her brother's plot, do you? Malcolm cleared her of any complicity."

"True, but her existence raises several possible scenarios as I see it. One. Someone else was involved and they'll want to eliminate her in case she knows something or want revenge for her involvement in bringing her brother's crimes to light. Two. That someone is as crazy as Bryant and will want to kill her for tainting her bloodline with Donald. Three. She stands in the way of someone taking over the clan, and thereby will need to be eliminated or convinced to support them. Four. Your preoccupation with her will drag you into her mess and get you killed."

Davis stiffened. Those scenarios had already occurred to him—all except the last. "I'm not preoccupied with her."

Greer stared at him, and then shrugged. "Suit yourself."

"Yes, I have been obsessed with tracking the scent of Donald's killer. She just happened to be the source."

Greer looked up as a hawk flew overhead but didn't say a word.

"I volunteered to accompany her back to the Euro clan because someone needed to. Malcolm can't. He's our leader and needed here, and besides he's a little busy with his new human mate. Owen's part of the ruling family and shouldn't be put in possible harm's way for no reason. Who else is going to volunteer? You? You want to volunteer? Be my guest."

Davis surged to his feet and stalked the length of the boulder and back. Greer wasn't exactly known for his social graces. He didn't have much use for people and wasn't shy about letting it show. He preferred remaining on the compound and only left if duty required him to do so. Malcolm had put him in charge of all security procedures there. Davis also handled any security duties off the compound when they arose, in order to spare his friend a task he disliked.

Propping his hands on his hips, he glared at the back of Greer's head.

Sure, her elusive scent had intrigued him. Of course, it did, but he had believed the scent belonged to Donald's killer. When they'd found her, he'd been stunned someone who appeared so small and delicate could be capable of such treachery. A normal reaction if you asked him. When the real culprit had been found, she'd been cleared of any involvement and free to go. Why in the world she wanted to return to the chaos of her clan was beyond him, but he supposed he could respect her loyalty to her clan.

He frowned at Greer who remained silent, fiddling with the piece of wood. A chill moved over his skin which had nothing to do with the cool breeze.

Her large, luminous eyes had been haunting his dreams since he'd first seen her. It was a natural response to dwell a little about the person he'd been tracking for weeks. The fact it turned out to be a woman had surprised him. And her face stuck in his brain. "I guess she's attractive if you like the fragile, quiet type."

Greer didn't respond.

Okay, she had a gentle beauty. Her light-blonde hair and ivory skin were pleasing to the eye. Her sweet little body had sent thoughts and images spiraling through his mind that had nothing to do with the crimes she had been accused of. Her eyes though, they were big, dark pools a man could drown in.

Davis spun away. He tilted his head back on his shoulders and stared up at the ever-lightening blue sky. The urge to howl rushed over him.

Damn it, he'd wanted her from the moment he'd laid eyes on her, and it had enraged him.

He hung his head and stared at the striations of rock beneath his toes. Who else had seen his reaction to

Bethany? What had given him away?

Crouching down next to Greer, he rested his forearms on his knees and hung his hands down in front of him.

Greer blew on the piece of wood to clear away debris. "Is she your mate?"

"I sure as hell hope not."

Chapter Two

The air-conditioned recycled air of the plane whooshed out of the vents as it blew over Bethany's head. The shades were drawn, and the lights dimmed in the cabin. The soft, leather, butter- colored lounge chair she reclined in provided comfort, but her eyes were wide open. Sleep proved elusive, despite her restless night, too many thoughts and worries coursing through her brain. What would she find when she returned home to Glasgow? Her cousin, Aaron, was the likely choice to rule the clan. He was next in line since her uncle and brother were both gone. Had Gregor, the clan's spiritual advisor, really challenged Aaron's right to rule? Could Malcolm Donovan have received misinformation? No. It was unlikely. He didn't strike her as the type of man to be unsure of his facts before presenting them to someone. She only had vague memories of Gregor and had only spoken to him a couple of times as far as she recalled—at official clan functions. Their conversations had been polite, with inane comments. Nothing of any true depth to gauge whether he would be a fit ruler.

She shifted in her seat and peered at her quiet companion beneath her lashes. Davis lounged on the row of seats to her right. His head was tilted back, eyes closed, hands resting on his flat abdomen, and his long, jean-clad legs were stretched out and crossed at the ankles.

7

Malcolm had insisted she needed an escort back to her clan. Although thankful for the private plane ride home, she couldn't help but wonder if Davis intended to spy on her as well as ensure she arrived safely back with her clan. An imaginary shrug accompanied her thoughts. It didn't matter if he was here to spy on her, there was nothing to find. She'd told them everything she knew. She had no secrets.

"There's food and drinks in the galley if you're hungry."

The rumble of words made her start, and she darted her gaze back up to his face. His eyes remained closed. Light brown hair rested in a haphazard disarray across his tan forehead. How had he known she was awake? Perhaps her restless thoughts had transferred to unconscious movements and given her away. Either that or he had felt her perusal of him.

"No, thank you. I'm not hungry or thirsty."

"Suit yourself."

Bethany nibbled on her bottom lip. Should she try to talk to him? His eyes were still closed. Did that mean he wanted to be left alone? He had spoken first however.

"If you've got something to say, spit it out."

"I…well…I wanted to thank you for escorting me home. It wasn't necessary, but I do appreciate the consideration."

Davis opened his hazel eyes, met her gaze, and shrugged. "Someone needed to, might as well be me."

Straightening in her seat, she lowered the footrest and placed her feet flat on the floor. "I could have gotten home without an escort. Perhaps not on a private plane, but I am perfectly capable of taking a commercial plane all by myself."

"Fly commercial? Why the hell would you want to do that? All those people jammed into one tiny space together, scents of perfume, cologne, stale food, body odor all colliding and piling up, the sheer volume of noise with all those people talking, breathing, and lord knows what else." He shuddered dramatically. "Gives me the urge to sneeze just thinking about it."

A slight smile twitched her lips. "It's not quite that bad."

"What are you doing flying commercial anyway? Your uncle was the leader of your clan. Surely you were able to enjoy some of the perks of being a member of the ruling family?"

"I have enjoyed the comfort and convenience of private planes the couple of times I accompanied my uncle, but when I travel by myself I fly commercial."

Davis shuddered. "Please tell me it was first class at least."

A light chuckle escaped her. "Mostly yes, although I have travelled coach a time or two as well. I do admit it was hard on my senses."

He gave a slight shake to his head, and a portion of brown hair fell forward across his forehead. He shoved it back.

"Why did you fly coach? Elsof that cheap?"

Bethany stiffened slightly and frowned. "It's not a matter of him being cheap. I wasn't one of his heirs or an executive with the company. I'm an engineer. My income doesn't always allow for extravagances like first class tickets."

"I would think for safety and security reasons alone, he should have provided you with secure, private transportation. You were his niece and therefore part of the ruling family. Besides, every member of the North American clan has access to one of the clan planes whenever they need it. Malcolm doesn't discriminate by heirs, blood, or position—every member of the clan is part of the family."

Gripping her knees with her hands, she stared at the floor. She didn't take offense at his words. Bethany felt certain he didn't ask them out of malice, but from general curiosity. The clans derived from the same planet, but just as many cultures who existed here on Earth, the Risharden clans had their differences too. Upon arrival, they had split into four different clans and for the most part they had remained somewhat isolated from one another over the centuries. The four leaders of the clans formed the council to try and keep the peace and ensure war never destroyed another planet. Keeping them isolated from one another across the globe had helped in the past, but modern times and the digital age made the philosophy increasingly difficult and perhaps antiquated. She had never even met a member of the South American clan until the meet and greet. They tended to keep to themselves. She had, however, encountered members of the Asian clan before. One of the trips she had accompanied her uncle on had been to India, where he had met with members from the Asian clan about some business deal they were both considering. He hadn't allowed her in the actual meeting. She had been there only for show. Her uncle felt strongly about presentation. Recently and unintentionally, she had become familiar with several members of the North American clan. If the clans didn't learn to evolve and to accept their differences and even grow to appreciate them, weren't they doomed to repeat past mistakes?

Crossing her legs, she rested her hands in her lap. "Your clan has many admirable qualities from what I've witnessed. There are certain traditions my clan has that I might wish were different, but change can be difficult, and many are resistant. No way of life is perfect, whether it be a person, family, clan, country, or culture. My clan is not perfect, but it is my clan, my family."

"Touché." Davis linked his fingers together, resting them on his stomach. "So, what's your plan when you get back?"

"My plan?"

"Yeah, your cousin and some other guy are battling over ruling the clan. Which side are you on?"

"Aaron is in line to rule the clan."

"But he's a dick, and not exactly leadership material. What about this Gregor guy? What's his story?"

Bethany opened her mouth but changed her mind. She couldn't refute his statement. Aaron had never demonstrated any of the qualities needed to run the clan. He was indecisive, impulsive, intolerant, entitled, and oft-times cruel. He was her cousin, but she wasn't blind to his faults. There was always the possibility the role of ruler could prompt him to become the leader the clan needed, but in her heart, she had doubts.

"I don't really know much about Advisor Heyes beyond he's the spiritual advisor for the clan. I would describe him as a quiet man. I would never have guessed he would challenge someone for ruler. He may be better suited, but I don't know him well enough to say."

His hazel gaze swept her from head to toe. "Sometimes it's the quiet ones you need to watch out for. They surprise you in the least expected ways."

For some unknown reason, heat stole over her skin. The more she thought about his words and the look in his eyes, the more her skin burned.

"I think I'll find some water. It seems I'm thirsty after all. The dry air on a plane makes it inevitable, I suppose." Bethany jumped to her feet and strode to the galley located toward the front of the plane. "Would you like me to get you something?"

Hearing nothing, she glanced over her shoulder.

He stood behind her.

She halted abruptly. "Oh, um."

"Decided I was hungry after all."

For a moment, all she could do was blink at him. "Oh, of course, I could bring you something."

A slight smile quirked at the corner of his mouth. Bethany couldn't stop staring.

"I'm already up."

Swinging back around, she marched into the galley and opened the refrigerator tucked under the counter. Filled to capacity with various drinks and food, she bent to grab a bottle of chilled water. Glancing at the bottle before she opened it, she contemplated holding it against her heated cheeks. Not wanting to draw further attention, she took a deep drink of the chilly water and wandered over to lean against the smooth wall separating the kitchen from the pilots flying the plane. Davis searched the small kitchen, opening cabinets and peering into the fridge.

"Decided on a sandwich, want one?"

Bethany glanced at the growing stack of ingredients piled on the counter and shook her head. The smell of meat and yeasty bread permeated the air. "No thank you."

The moments ticked by while he made a sandwich large enough to sustain her for days. She took the opportunity to study him, as she'd always been a bit too preoccupied the past few times she had encountered him. Being on death's door after your brother almost murdered you could do that. And being suspected of killing Donald, finding out Bryant's full treachery, and losing her uncle, she hadn't thought of Davis as anything other than someone who, perhaps rightfully so, blamed her for his friend's death.

He was tall. She had noticed his height before, when he loomed over the cot she had huddled on— terrified and sick. Although most people were taller than her, he topped her by at least a foot. His hands captured her gaze. His movements were quick and efficient, smooth, no hesitation.

Her gaze travelled up to his profile. He was an extraordinarily attractive man, in a disheveled sort of way. Not polished like the men she was accustomed to. Of course, she had recognized his handsomeness before, but in a distracted manner at the back of her mind. Now, it was just the two of them standing here without all of the other distractions. She glanced down at the borrowed clothes she wore. A black silk blouse and linen skirt, both high quality, but a couple of sizes too large for her frame, made her feel like a little girl playing dress up with her mother's clothes. Something she'd never had the opportunity to do.

A pain in her chest, and a sting at the back of her

eyes made her take another sip of water as she bent slightly to stare out the window of the plane. Pillows of white, painted on a light blue background as far as the eye could see. So many times as a child she would lie on the grass and stare at the sky picturing the clouds as fanciful shapes and creatures. Such a different view from above than below.

The metallic opening of a can and the fizzing of a carbonated drink jerked her gaze back to Davis. He leaned against the counter, the remains of his sandwich in one hand and a soda in the other. He glanced at her over the top of the can as he took a sip.

"Worried about your reception?"

Her brow wrinkled. She hadn't really considered her clan's reaction. There were probably those who would blame her for her brother's actions, and probably some would consider her disloyal for condemning his deeds and telling Malcolm of his crimes. A traditional mindset pervaded her clan. Her uncle had held the firm belief, his word and only his was the final say. He had skirted the rules with the council, only sharing what he deemed necessary. Perhaps with new leadership they would begin to accept change more readily while still respecting their customs. Sadness had gripped her at the news of her uncle's death, but true grieving had remained elusive. Maybe the tragic events of late had provided a buffer, or maybe it was because they had never been close. She was a female, and therefore beneath his notice. She sighed. Perhaps she was being too harsh. Her feelings toward her family members were conflicted lately.

She slightly shook her head. "No. People will believe and think what they want. I can't worry about their opinions."

Davis raised his can in the air. "Exactly."

As she stepped forward to put her empty bottle in the recycling bin, the plane hit a spot of turbulence. Her shoes, being one size too large, didn't provide the stability she needed to keep her balance. Stumbling, she threw an arm out to grasp the counter.

Instead of the sharp, cool, metal counter she had anticipated, her hand encountered a solid warmth of solid muscle.

Davis wrapped an arm around her waist and held her steady against his body.

Bethany grasped his hard bicep with one hand and clutched the water bottle between them with the other. The crackling of hollow plastic and the quiet hum of the plane engines were the only sounds she heard, as she stared straight ahead at his chest.

The light blue fabric of his shirt had been washed many times. The soft, thin material stretched across the muscles of his upper body. A slight woodsy scent emanated from his skin. A fluttering of awareness invaded her abdomen.

She peeked upward. Her gaze encountered his tan throat, stubborn chin, full lips, strong nose, and collided with his piercing eyes.

Abruptly, he dropped his arm and stepped away. "The turbulence seems to have passed."

She grabbed the counter and gripped the edge, but her gaze stayed riveted on him as Davis sauntered away.

Had it stopped? Then why did the world feel so off kilter?

Chapter Three

Stepping off the plane onto the hard tarmac, a calm washed over Bethany. She raised her face to the familiar gray-blue sky and took a deep breath. Despite the cacophony of sounds from planes and other vehicles arriving and departing and people milling about, she easily tuned it all out, so it sounded like a distant, low hum. She experienced the connection every time she returned from a trip. She was home.

She'd always enjoyed travelling, experiencing new sights and people, but her heart resided here in Scotland. Her spirit lighter, she crossed to Davis standing several feet away.

Bethany smiled and held out her hand. "Thank you very much for escorting me home."

He glanced at her hand briefly but didn't take it. "You're not home yet." He gestured to a dark sedan pulling up. "Here's our ride."

Trailing after him as fast as her borrowed shoes would allow as he stalked toward the car, she raised her voice to be heard. "I'm sure Mr. Donovan didn't intend for you to take me all the way to my door. I assure you, your duty is complete."

Ignoring her, he took possession of the car, tossed his duffel bag into the back, and climbed into the driver's seat.

Bethany hesitated only for a moment before getting

in the passenger seat and buckling her seatbelt. She hadn't been worried before about her arrival home, but now tension tightened her shoulders. How would they react to her companion? Permission to enter the compound was not granted lightly. They could refuse him entry. "If you insist on going, I should drive. I'm more familiar with the area, and most importantly, accustomed to driving on the correct side of the road."

Davis barely spared her a glance before stepping on the gas, sending her back against her seat. She gripped the armrest as her foot pressed on the nonexistent brake on her side of the car.

After exiting the airport and surviving, her clenched muscles relaxed. Although he drove much faster than she preferred, he drove competently and thankfully on the correct side of the road.

Historic buildings juxtaposed with modern sculptures and structures sped by her window. Cranes were hard at work in the ever-expanding city. The green hills surrounding the urban area were drenched in clouds. The teeming streets were filled with traffic and people bustling along the busy pavements. A street performer stood on a corner playing the bagpipes for wandering tourists. Pigeons combed the plaza searching for crumbs. Happiness bloomed inside her at the familiar views. There had been moments recently when she thought she would never see them again.

As he proceeded down the street to the main entrance of her clan's compound, he slowed the car and glanced her way. "Remember, you don't know what you're arriving home to. Be alert."

"Mr. Davis, I appreciate your concern, but I will be fine."

"My last name is Campbell. Davis is my first name."

"Oh, Mr. Campbell then."

"Just call me Davis."

"Thank you, and of course, call me Bethany."

"Great, now that the pleasantries are out of the way, would you please focus on the matter at hand. Your clan is in the middle of a coup. Your brother almost started a war with my clan, and he's probably the one presumed responsible for murdering your uncle, and oh yeah, he embezzled from the company. You don't know what kind of greeting we'll get."

Straightening her shoulders and pursing her lips, she angled her head to glance at him. "If you're concerned about your safety, you can simply let me out here. I can walk the block to the entrance."

Davis briefly glared at her and continued down the street. The towering brownish gray stone wall surrounding her compound loomed ahead. It spanned the size of several city blocks, all enclosed within the wall. It bordered the River Clyde on one side, which helped to facilitate their shipping business.

A guard stepped out of the guard shack next to the closed metal gate as they pulled up. There were two guards positioned inside the gate facing the entrance. The compound's wall made it difficult to see much beyond the gate.

Bethany ducked her head and leaned toward Davis. She needed to speak to the guard approaching the driver's side. Davis lowered the window, keeping his gaze on the advancing guard and the two beyond the gate.

"Hi Walter, it's nice to see you. How is Colleen?"

The guard stared at Davis before glancing at Bethany and giving her a small smile and a nod. "She's doing well, Lady Bethany. She claims our wee one is doing somersaults in her womb. It's an immense pleasure to see you come home safe and sound."

Clearly hesitant to grant Davis entrance to the compound, Walter glanced at him again. Had he been ordered to forbid anyone from entering?

She smiled widely and tried to ease the way. "I have Malcolm Donovan and his clan to thank for that. Mr. Campbell has very kindly escorted me home to see I arrive safely."

Walter nodded. "Welcome home, Lady Bethany." He stepped back to wave a hand at the other guards to open the gate.

As the gate slid open and the guards stepped out of the way, she smiled and nodded at them one by one as Davis maneuvered past. "I'd like to go to my flat. It's at the far end of the compound, past the square and company headquarters." Changing into her own clothes and taking a few moments to herself was foremost on her mind.

A wide cobblestone street ran down the center of the compound with smaller roads branching off to separate the rows of buildings. It was one of the few remaining cobblestone streets that remained intact in the city. A large, square plaza occupied the center of the compound. In the warmer months they sometimes held clan gatherings there. Tall ash trees full of leaves shielded the pink, white, and blue flowers circling their trunks and anchored the four corners of the square. Stone benches dotted the perimeter of the common area.

Passing the square, she looked ahead to the tallest building on the compound. A tower of metal and glass housed the company headquarters and clan offices.

Aaron, surrounded by six guards, stood on the street, in front of the building.

"Looks like your cousin has other ideas. Do you want me to stop or go around them?"

She focused her gaze and studied her cousin. Her eyesight was one of her strongest senses, along with her hearing. A tailored gray suit with a black striped tie garbed his tall, thin frame. She could not recall a time when she had seen him wear anything but a suit. His dark hair was slicked back, and his chin was raised toward the sky. A familiar scowl sharpened his angular features. Bethany sighed. "Stop, please. Aaron becomes unpleasant if his wishes are ignored."

"Are you afraid of him?" The question surprised her, and for a split second she hesitated.

Davis stared at her expression intently, waiting for her response. He didn't slow the car. If she gave the slightest indication she feared him, then he was swinging the car around and heading straight back to the airport. He saw no reason to continue this charade and endanger her any more. Her family had harmed her enough.

"No, of course not. Please stop."

He braked abruptly, tightening the seatbelt against his chest, and the car stopped within inches of the front guards. Bethany gasped and gripped her seat with both hands. Davis didn't take his eyes off the guards or Aaron. Their widened eyes and Aaron's small jump backward did little to assuage the feelings churning in his gut.

Bethany unbuckled her seatbelt and grasped the door handle. "That was completely unnecessary."

"Not to me."

Davis exited the car and strode around the back to hold her door as she stood up. She frowned at him and walked toward the guards, pasting a smile on her face which didn't reach her eyes.

"Hello, everyone. I'm so happy to be home. It's kind of you to come welcome me home, Aaron." She peeked to the side to meet the gaze of a guard standing in the back. "Ned, I didn't see you there. How is your mother?"

The red-headed guard smiled, but before he could reply Aaron made a slicing motion with his hand. "Do you have any idea the problems you have caused with your disappearing act?" He took a step toward her. "Do you know what your brother has done to this clan?"

Davis positioned himself to stand in front of her rather than at her side. His fists clenched. If the bastard made one move toward her, he would take him out, guards or not.

Bethany leaned around Davis and peered up at him. As soon as he glanced down to meet her gaze, she frowned at him, and then fixed her gaze on Aaron. "Unfortunately, I'm well aware of my brother's crimes, Aaron. He was also responsible for my prolonged absence. Now, why don't we have this discussion inside, in private?"

Aaron stiffened. "We will have this discussion where and when I say. I am the ruler of this clan, and you will do as you are instructed."

"Way I heard it, rule over this clan was still undecided, Aaron." Davis smirked as Aaron's face turned a mottled red.

Bethany tapped his arm and moved to step around him. He shifted and kept her behind him. There wasn't a chance he was putting her in harm's way. Her cousin was a powder keg just waiting to go off. Bethany's petite stature was probably just the right size for him to vent his rage on, too.

"*Lord* Aaron, and I am the rightful heir to the clan." He somehow managed to puff himself up even more while he spouted the dictate.

Barely resisting the urge to outright laugh in his face, Davis snorted. "Yeah, you're not my Lord anything, and as far as the council knows your claim to the clan has been challenged."

Bethany yanked on his arm.

Davis glanced down first at her hand and then at her face. He cocked one eyebrow. Did she really think he would bow down to her cousin?

"I'm sure Mr. Campbell didn't mean any disrespect." She ignored Davis' grunt and plowed on. "He and the North American clan have been extremely helpful to me. They saved my life and kept me safe from Bryant. He was kind enough to accompany me home. Now that I am here, I'm sure he's in a hurry to be on his way back to his clan. So why don't you and I go inside, and Mr. Campbell can leave?"

Davis glared down at the top of her head. He had no intention of going anywhere. He wasn't leaving her alone in this pit of vipers.

Aaron gave a sharp, single nod and glared at the both of them.

Wanted to get rid of him, did he? Too bad. Davis folded his arms over his chest and didn't move.

Bethany faced him with a brittle smile on her face. "Davis, thank you very much for everything. I'm delivered, safe and sound, and it's time for you to return to your clan. Please convey my sincere gratitude once again to Malcolm Donovan and the rest of your clan. I'm forever in their debt."

"Laying it on a bit thick, aren't you? I'm not ready to go yet. Malcolm wanted me to make sure you got home safely, and from your dear cousin's reception, I'm hardly getting any warm and fuzzies to reassure me."

The cloying scent of cologne assaulted his sinuses before he heard the approaching tread of footsteps.

"Lady Bethany, I was delighted to hear of your safe return."

They all turned to the new arrival. A tall, thin man with white hair and a goatee approached them. He wore a full-length purple robe in the tradition of Risharden spiritual leaders. This must be Gregor, the challenger to the clan.

Bethany smiled and inclined her head. "Thank you, Advisor Heyes. I am happy to be home."

At a similar height, the amiable man smiled in Davis' direction. "And who might you be, young man?"

"Oh, please forgive me, this is Davis Campbell from the North American clan."

"Ah, how nice. Many years ago, I met your former leader, James Donovan—your current Lord's father if I am not mistaken. A fierce man, fierce, but fair."

"Yes." Davis recalled the towering leader the same way. He had played the role of a distant father figure to him with Davis having grown up without a father of his own.

The advisor stood with his hands clasped in front of him, and with a congenial smile on his face. No guards accompanied him. Was he still challenging for leadership of the clan? He sensed no hostility emanating from the man, but a pleasant smile could hide a conniving heart. Just look at Bryant. He had been amicable enough too when he first met him, and he ended up being a murderous bastard.

The man tilted his head inquiringly. "Will you be staying with us long?"

"No, he—"

"I haven't decided yet." When Davis interrupted Bethany, she glared up at him. He ignored her.

"Well, I hope you enjoy your stay. If I can be of any assistance, please do not hesitate to seek me out."

Aaron sputtered. "He's not staying, and you have no authority, Advisor Heyes."

Davis glanced between the two. This should be interesting.

"That remains to be seen, Lord Aaron. It is up to the clan to decide who has authority and who does not. In the meantime, what possible objection could you have to his presence? Has he committed some crime I am not aware of?"

Aaron's face started turning shades again, and Davis fought a smile. The guy really needed to learn how to handle his emotions.

Bethany curled her toes inside her borrowed shoes and fought the urge to throw her hands up in the air and walk away. They were behaving like overgrown children. Instead, she took a deep breath of the damp air emanating from the river and strove to smooth over the rough emotions flying about.

"He's committed no crime. Davis and his clan saved me."

"Well then, that's settled. He is your guest, and we must extend him our hospitality. After you get settled in, I would like to meet with you, Lady Bethany, at your convenience."

"Of course."

"What for?" Aaron demanded.

"That is between Lady Bethany and me, is it not? Good day."

The advisor bowed slightly before marching away toward the temple, located beyond the square. She looked back at Aaron still surrounded by guards. His pinched features and clenched fists did not bode well for rational conversation.

"Aaron, if it is all right with you, I would like to go to my flat. Could we continue our conversation later, or is there something pressing you would like to discuss immediately?"

Aaron glared at her a moment. "One hour, in the conference room." He spun around and almost plowed into the guards at his back. "Move, imbeciles." The front guards followed after, giving Bethany a slight bow. She smiled at them.

An hour reprieve. At least it was something.

As she marched over to the car, she noticed a few of her fellow clan members milling about. No doubt they were hoping for some juicy tidbits of gossip. Dropping her shoulders over the unkind thought, she tossed an absent smile in their direction before climbing into the vehicle. Davis sauntered over to the driver's side and eased into the seat. Bethany gave him a sideways glance.

What on Earth was she going to do about him?

The car shot forward, but this time she was prepared and had grasped the door handle. Her homecoming now marred by her cousin's ambush, she valiantly tried to relax and appreciate the sight of her home.

Pointing a finger at the turn for her lane, she leaned forward as he made the left-hand turn. Her flat was located on the river side of the compound. She couldn't actually see the river from her flat though, only if she went up to the roof. And if she peered over the back-left corner. The lane was paved with cobblestones as well, a narrower version of the main thoroughfare. A line of stone buildings ran the length on either side. Wide stretches of pavement edged between the lane and buildings creating a generous walkway. Some were single dwellings, but most on this lane, like hers, were divided up into multiple flats. Each door was painted a distinct color to distinguish from one another as they were all the same brown streaked gray stone. Her door held the color of bluebells, her favorite color.

"That one, there."

Davis parked the car. She hesitated to see what he would do. She had learned her lesson regarding making assumptions about if and when he would leave. He opened his door, so she got out and walked to the pavement. He wasn't leaving. He really did intend to stay awhile.

Sighing, Bethany decided to put off any confrontation with him. She had enough to worry about with her cousin and Advisor Heyes. She only had a brief time before she had to meet with them.

The clip clop of hooves striking the cobblestones

echoed down the lane. A pure white horse with flowing mane and tail pranced toward them. Inclining its regal head as it passed them, the horse continued on its way.

Davis glanced at her, and she smiled. "That was Mrs. Evanwood. She lives down by the river."

"I suppose a horse doesn't raise too much of a notice in the city."

Shrugging slightly, she gazed after the horse. It was a form that had more freedom. To any human they would only see a pretty horse, a common enough sight. Only another Risharden would be able to recognize it as one of their own kind. A Risharden had an instinctual sense. She used to believe the intelligence hidden behind the eyes revealed their true form, but she had come across some animals she knew to be only animals, and their eyes held the same intelligence.

"Bethany! Bethany!"

She whirled around to see Colin racing toward her down the pavement. He was a little boy who lived in one of the flats farther up the lane. His carrot colored hair fell over his forehead as he skidded to a stop in front of her. His bright blue eyes were shining—emphasizing the delightful freckles sprinkled across his nose.

Laughing, she bent and gave him a noisy kiss on the cheek. He promptly wiped his cheek with the back of his hand, leaving a smudge of dirt behind.

"What have you been up to?"

"Guess what?"

He didn't wait for her to speak but plowed on. "My Dad told me one of our ancestors was a dragon! I could be one, too!"

Colin had become preoccupied with guessing what

form he might shift into when he was old enough. Even though he had several years to wait, he constantly quizzed the members of his family about the possibilities. His mother would affectionately smile at him while he *blethered* on. Although it appeared to increase the chances, family members' forms did not guarantee what shape one would be able to shift into. Look at her, for instance. She was an owl, yet her brother had been a lion and a gryphon. He had been one of the few able to transform into more than one shape, at least that she knew of. Her mother had been a swan, and her father a lion. She supposed the argument could be made a correlation existed. With the exception of her father, they were all flying creatures, and Bryant had taken a little bit of both their parents.

Bouncing from one foot to the other, Colin beamed up at her.

"Do you know that I recently met a dragon shifter?"

His mouth dropped open, and his eyes grew wide. "*Aye right!*"

Bethany nodded. "Yes, I did. The leader of the North American clan, Malcolm Donovan, is a dragon shifter."

"That is *pure barry!*"

"Yes, it is fine. In fact, this is Mr. Campbell, and he is also from the North American clan." She gestured to Davis standing behind her with his thumbs resting in the front belt loops of his jeans.

Colin peered around her and gawked at him. "Are you a dragon shifter, too?"

Davis chuckled and shook his head. "'Fraid not. I'm a wolf."

"*Braw*."

Davis raised an eyebrow and looked at her.

She smiled. "It means he likes it." Colin's thick accent heavily doused with colloquial terms might be hard to grasp for someone unaccustomed to hearing them.

Colin shuffled closer to stand between them. "I could be a good wolf. I like to run around a lot. My Mam and Da say I run them ragged." He wrinkled his nose. "Though I would like to fly." His face brightened. "I could be both! That happens, right?"

Bethany grinned. "I suppose anything is possible."

"I better skedaddle. Mam made tarts this morning. Brendon will eat them all."

Watching him run off, her mood was much improved, but then he always had a positive effect on her disposition. He was a delightful handful. She looked back at Davis watching him scamper off. "Brendon is his little brother."

"I guessed it was something along those lines. Neighborhood kid?"

"Yes, they live up at the corner. In the past year he's become a tad obsessed with guessing what he will shift into when he's old enough."

"I went through that stage, also. Didn't you?"

Shrugging, she climbed the stairs to her building. "Not really. There wasn't anyone to question about shifting. I grew up in the Highlands with only my nanny."

Bethany opened the blue door and glanced over her shoulder. "Were your parents wolves?"

"Yes, both of them, so I guess my fate was pretty much sealed. Didn't stop me from imagining being a dragon though."

She started the long climb up the three flights of stairs to her flat. "It makes perfect sense considering the leaders of your clan are a dragon shifter family."

"Yeah, well, they were more my family. I never knew my parents."

Pausing on the stairs, she stopped and turned back to him. "Something we have in common."

"That's not the only thing we have in common."

"Oh?" She stared up into his hazel eyes as he paused on the stairs next to her. What else could they have in common?

"We're both loyal to our clans. That confrontation your cousin subjected you to has to show you what kind of dictator he would be. You really want him ruling your clan?"

Bethany sighed and ascended the stairs. Ah yes, back to her reality and the clamor of who she would support. She understood why the outcome was important to the other clans, of course it was, but it wasn't like her opinion held much sway. Why all of a sudden did everyone appear to care what she thought?

Chapter Four

"Malcolm, I need to stay here and keep an eye on things." As soon as Bethany had excused herself, he'd taken out his phone to call Malcolm.

"Explain."

Davis rolled his shoulders and walked to the window of Bethany's glorified apartment in a stone building smack dab in the middle of a row of similar buildings. The size of a large bedroom back home, he supposed it held a certain old-world charm if you liked that sort of a thing. "Something doesn't feel right. The clan hasn't decided on a new ruler yet. I met Advisor Gregor Heyes, friendly enough on the surface, he's pushing for some kind of vote. I don't have all the details yet. Aaron is the same dickhead we dealt with before, demanding he's the rightful ruler, and trying to bully everyone else into accepting it."

Silence echoed over the connection. He glanced toward the bathroom where Bethany had disappeared to refresh herself, before her meeting with Aaron. The shower was still on. Her delicate scent filled the tiny space.

"What's Bethany's role in all of this?"

"Not entirely sure. Aaron greeted her surrounded by guards when we arrived. He wasn't exactly welcoming to his little cousin. She's supposed to meet with him in less than an hour. The advisor greeted her and was extremely courteous, and he also wants to meet with her."

"Both want her support. Who do you think she's backing?"

"Not entirely sure. I asked her the same question before we arrived."

"What do you need from me?"

"Like I said, I need to stick around a bit. Aaron, of course, wants me gone. Advisor Heyes welcomed me to stay."

"And Bethany?"

Davis snorted. "Yeah, well, the little peacemaker tried to get rid of me when I didn't kowtow to Aaron and the advisor. I don't think she fully realizes the precarious position she and her clan are in right now."

"On the contrary, I am quite aware, which is why I don't see the need to make the matter worse by antagonizing everyone around me."

Davis slowly swiveled his head to meet Bethany's glare. She stood in the open doorway to the bathroom with her arms wrapped tightly around her waist. Her dark gaze pinned on him. She'd changed into a blue dress. It accentuated her tiny waist, skimming just below her knees, and allowing him an appreciative view of her trim legs. Her pursed lips only accentuated the pink little bow of her mouth, making him imagine what it might be like to grab a taste.

An amused chuckle sounded in his ear. "She doesn't sound very happy with you, Davis. Are you sure you want to stay?"

"Yeah, I'm sure."

"All right. I'll notify both Aaron and Advisor Heyes as well as the other council members that you are there on council business to advise us on the state of their clan and its leadership."

"You can do that?"

"An unstable clan is dangerous for us all. It's the council's mandate to ensure peace among the clans. You will keep us apprised of the situation, and any cause for concern."

"Understood."

"And Davis, watch your back." Malcolm disconnected, and Davis slipped his phone into his pocket.

He sighed and braced himself for the female tirade he was sure was headed his way. She hadn't moved from her position in the doorway. He turned, facing her fully, and folded his arms across his chest. *Fire away, sweetheart.*

She glanced away and walked over to the small galley style kitchen against the right side of the apartment. The cabinets were painted a cheery pale yellow.

"Do you want something to eat or drink?"

"Depends, you plan to poison it?"

She glanced over her shoulder briefly before turning back to the kitchen. "Still too new for that particular joke."

Davis winced. "Right, sorry."

"I'm making tea. Would you like some, or something else? I'm not sure how long this meeting with Aaron will last."

After filling a little blue teapot and placing it on the stove, she reached into the cabinet and pulled out a white tea cup trimmed in pink flowers.

"I'll take a coffee if you have it."

She nodded, and he ambled over to the small two-person wooden table situated against the wall next to the kitchen and sat down on one of the matching stools. He'd glanced around the apartment when they first arrived to make sure it was secure. The one bedroom wasn't much larger than a walk-in closet, and the bathroom was only large enough to hold a shower stall, toilet, and pedestal sink. This room held the kitchen on one side and a couch, chair, and bookshelves on the other. Spacious it was not. The entire place could fit inside what he remembered of her brother's master bedroom.

There were no photographs hanging on the walls or sitting on the shelves. A painting of a small white house by a lake hung on the wall next to him over the table.

Bethany placed the coffee down in front of him. "Do you take cream or sugar?"

"No, black is fine, thanks."

She took her seat across from him and clasped her tea cup in her hands, staring down at the table. Her pale blonde hair was tucked behind her ears, where it formed a curly halo around her head.

Raising her cup to her lips, she gently blew across the top before taking a sip. A slight pink sheen shone from her pursed lips. Her lashes were darker and fuller. She'd put some makeup on, but not much. For whom?

He paused in the middle of taking a drink of his coffee. The dark aroma circled beneath his nose. Was she interested in someone here at her clan?

Wait, no. She had met Donald at a meet and greet, so *she had* been looking to meet someone. He'd never understood the appeal of the meet and greets. A bunch of desperate Rishardens getting together hoping to find their mate among those gathered. He'd been surprised Donald had attended one, but he supposed if you were searching for your mate and were out of options, then the meet and greet provided a possibility at least. But how many had actually ever discovered their mate that way? The gatherings were held under a veil of secrecy because of the stigma attached to clans intermingling, so there wasn't exactly a newsletter published announcing the statistics, not any he was aware of anyway. And if they did find their mate, how did they overcome the obstacles which would then surface? Being from different clans, one of them would have to leave their family and join the other's or both go somewhere else entirely, leaving their clans behind. Not something he could ever see himself doing.

Davis took a drink of the steaming brew and set down his cup. Strong and hot, just the way he preferred his coffee. Why anyone wanted to mar the perfection of coffee with all those additives advertised these days, he did not understand.

And he didn't understand Bethany. Where was the tirade? She couldn't possibly think her silence served as a punishment—he couldn't be that lucky.

"I think we need to clear the air."

Ah, here it comes. He leaned back on his stool and crossed his arms over his chest.

Bethany placed her cup down and folded her hands in her lap before looking up at him.

"I am very grateful for all that you and your clan have done for me. I realize I owe you a debt. However, that does not mean I will be used as a tool to spy on my own clan."

Davis couldn't help but laugh. A spy? No one

would dream of using her as a spy. Spies needed to blend in, not stick out in the middle of a crowd. She was too damn beautiful to be a spy.

"I don't appreciate being laughed at. I'm serious, as much as I owe you, I won't do anything to harm my clan."

"I don't recall anyone asking you to."

"I heard part of your conversation. Mr. Donovan wants you to stay here and keep tabs on my clan. What is that if not spying?"

"It's making sure this little coup going on in your clan doesn't escalate into a full out war." Davis leaned toward her. "It's keeping your cute little butt out of the line of fire, or has it not occurred to you that your dear cousin and Advisor Heyes want to meet with you to garner your support. How kindly do you think the loser is going to take it when you make your decision?"

She stared at him with those pink pursed lips. The urge to lift her off the stool and into his lap and plant a kiss on those lips had fire spreading through his veins.

He lurched off the stool and stalked to the chipped porcelain sink. Placing his cup in it, he gripped the edge of the counter and kept his back to the little temptation.

"You're not my bodyguard, Davis. I keep telling you, you're not responsible for me. I can handle my cousin and Advisor Heyes."

He spun around. "Like you dealt with your brother?"

Bethany stiffly rose from the stool. She smoothed the front of her dress and gave him a withering look. "That was uncalled for." She turned her back on him and started walking toward her bedroom.

Davis winced and pinched the bridge of his nose.

Damn it. Why couldn't she react to things like he expected. Scream at him, throw something, anything but the hurt, *how could you* look.

"I'm sorry."

Stopping at the door, she looked back at him.

"Look, no one expects you to spy or betray your clan, okay? I'm just here to make sure things don't get out of control. I'll simply be reporting to the council. It's all above board. Your clan will know exactly why I'm here."

Placing her hand on the doorknob, she nodded. "You will need a place to stay while you're here. There are guest suites in the main building reserved for visiting dignitaries. I'll arrange for you to have one when we go to the meeting with Aaron."

She started to enter her bedroom, but stopped again, and glanced back. "I've dealt with contrary men all my life. My brother wasn't contrary; he was evil. I didn't see it, and that's something I will live with the rest of my days. I suppose I can learn to deal with one more contrary man for the length of your stay."

Bethany walked into her room and closed the door with a quiet snap.

Davis leaned back against the counter and folded his arms. Well, it looked like the little owl had teeth after all.

Chapter Five

Stress pounded on the front of Bethany's skull. She rotated her neck and shrugged her shoulders, trying to relieve some of the tension that had wrapped her body and taken root. The late afternoon sun shone overly bright to her weary eyes as she exited the headquarters. Her meetings with Aaron, and then Advisor Heyes, had only added to the questions ricocheting around her brain rather than providing any answers. Both wanted to lead, and both wanted, or in her cousins' case, demanded her support.

"Bethany!"

Recognition caused her to pause and swivel in the direction of the voices. She smiled and shot her hand up to wave at her two closest friends.

Kate and Celeste closed the distance separating them from Bethany with a stilted jog, despite their three-inch heels and snug skirts. They enveloped her in a three-way hug. The three of them had bonded once discovering none of them had been raised on the compound. Fitting into the fiercely closed clan had not been easy. Finding friends to rely on who were in the same position had drawn them together and enabled them to help one another find their place.

"We heard you were back and rushed over right away. We've been so worried. How are you? Is it true? Did Bryant really do all those horrible things?"

"Celeste, take a breath, give her a minute." Kate gently squeezed Bethany's arm and leaned her head against hers briefly before straightening. "Why don't we go back to my place. We can have some wine and pry all the details out of you in comfort."

Bethany cast a furtive glance toward Davis. He stood about ten feet away with his thumbs resting in the front belt loops of his jeans. She'd been so intent on getting a breath of fresh air after the meeting she'd completely forgotten to show him to the guest suite. She glanced back at her friends and forced a smile to her lips. "That sounds like a wonderful idea, but I need to take care of something first. Does meeting in an hour work for you?"

Kate followed her gaze to Davis and grinned. She sauntered over to him and tilted her dark head to the side. A thick tendril of black hair drifted across her cheek. Her blue-eyed gaze wandered from the top of his head all the way to his cowboy boots and back up again. Bracelets jangled when she cocked her hip and propped her hands on her hips. "Who are you?"

Celeste gave a sharp intake of breath. Bethany barely restrained the sigh itching to come out. Celeste gave an artful toss of her dirty blonde hair and tottered over to Davis and Kate. Realizing introductions were unavoidable, Bethany followed along. "This is Davis Campbell. He escorted me home from the North American Clan. These are my friends Kate and Celeste."

He briefly shook Kate's hand as she held it out to him. Celeste, accustomed to men kissing her hand, dangled it palm down in front of his face. Bethany held her breath hoping he wouldn't insult her friend. Celeste tended to be sensitive, and she didn't want to see her hurt. Davis glanced at the offered hand, grasped and released it quickly. He stuffed both hands in the front pockets of his jeans as if he was afraid they would latch on to them. Knowing her friends, they probably would, and stuffing them in his trousers wasn't a guarantee to stop them. He stared at Bethany, his eyes entreating her to do something. She supposed her friends could be a bit overenthusiastic.

Bethany took a step closer. "I need to get him set up in one of the guest suites. He will be staying here on council business. I'll see both of you in about an hour." Perfume wafted from each as she kissed both of them on their cheeks before walking back toward the double glass doors of the headquarters. Davis arrived first and held the door. After stepping inside, she glanced back to see her friends standing on the pavement watching them. She sent a brief wave and smile in their direction before addressing the guards at the chest high security desk. "I apologize. I neglected to get Mr. Campbell set up in a guest suite. He will need a keycard."

"Of course, Lady Bethany. One moment, please."

Clasping her hands in front of her, she smiled politely and stared at the back of the computer as he checked for authorization. She hoped the request had been entered, otherwise she would need to speak to her cousin or Advisor Heyes again to have the matter cleared up. Her stomach churned. She didn't want to speak to either one of them again so soon. If she wasn't careful this whole situation would give her an ulcer.

"Here we are. It will be just another minute."

She listened distractedly while the guard gave Davis instructions, took his picture, and handed him a keycard.

"Thank you. I'll show him to his suite."

"Do you require an escort, Lady Bethany?"

"No. Thank you."

The guard nodded and glanced at Davis a moment before returning to his work.

Walking to the elevators, she smiled and nodded at her clan members as they passed. Once they were in the elevator, she faced Davis. "I'm not certain whether he explained or not, but your keycard will only access specific floors. You will need an escort to visit any restricted floors."

"He explained, but I'm familiar with the process."

Swinging back to the metal doors, she stared at the smudged fingerprints on shiny metal. A low hum accompanied the climb up to his floor. She wanted to get him settled quickly and then be on her way. Perhaps she should make excuses to her friends and visit another time. Her heart just wasn't in it today. A chime sounded, signaling their arrival at his floor.

"Here we are." The doors opened, and they proceeded down the hall. "I believe you are the only visitor currently, so the entire floor is empty." She stopped in front of a set of double wooden doors and stepped back for him to use his keycard and enter.

The doors opened into a spacious room with a wide expanse of glass showcasing the view of the River Clyde. If you walked closer to the window, you could gaze down onto the shipyard. She emitted a slight sigh of relief. She had been concerned he would be put in a small room used for the visitor's bodyguards or other staff as a sign of disrespect. Thankfully, someone had the foresight not to further insult the North American clan. Sadly, she doubted it had been her cousin who made the decision. Perhaps the Advisor, or could one of the guards have made the assumption on his own? Regardless, she was thankful.

Davis inspected the entire suite, including the various rooms opening off the main room. She waited patiently by the entrance and gazed out the window at the winding path of the river.

"This is quite the pad."

"I'm glad you approve. If you need anything, you can use the phone on the wall here." She pointed to the phone next to her. "They'll even help you with dining options outside the compound if you desire."

"Anxious to get rid of me?"

Bethany blinked. "No, of course not. Is there something else I can help you with?"

Davis walked into the small kitchenette which opened off the main living area and peered into the minifridge. "Looks like it's fully stocked. What would you like?"

"Nothing for me, thank you."

He opened a can of soda and handed her a bottle of water. "You'll want to hydrate before you go drinking wine with your friends."

She wanted to refuse, but she was in fact thirsty, so she accepted the bottle and murmured, "Thank you." Her mouth was dry and tasted a bit stale. Perhaps the icy water would help revive her a bit as well.

"Have a seat. You have time before you need to meet with your friends."

Taking a sip of water, she followed him to the couches by the windows and sat on the edge of the couch across from him.

Davis took a long drink from the soda can and rested his ankle on his opposite knee. He rested the can on his bent knee and stared at her.

Bethany took another sip and waited for him to speak. He probably wanted to discuss the meeting and question her about her intentions. She wasn't in the mood for another interrogation. Aaron had made her feel like she was on trial during their meeting, making her go over every detail of her experience in the States. She had stared at the long glass table in the center of the room and silently counted the minutes until it would end. He hadn't asked her to sit. Standing in front of the wide window with the sun outlining him through the tinted glass, he had directed her to limit her contact with Advisor Heyes and demanded she give him a full report of any meeting she had with him. After making his dictates, he had ended the meeting rather abruptly and walked out of the room, not saying a word to Davis who had been waiting outside the conference room.

Thankfully, Advisor Heyes had been less confrontational and briefer. Still, the result remained the same—they both wanted her support. The Advisor simply approached it in a more diplomatic manner. He had called for a clan wide vote to choose who would rule the clan.

Davis watched as Bethany took another sip of water and stared at the floor. Her dress teased the edges of her knees as she sat on the couch with her feet and knees firmly planted together. The woman certainly didn't mind the silences. Apparently, she felt no need to fill the silences with chatter. When she had stepped out of the conference room after her meeting with her dick of a cousin, the exhausted and defeated expression on her face gave him the urge to plant his fist in her cousin's face. She'd silently stood in the doorway while her cousin and his guards disappeared into the elevator. Advisor Heyes had sedately stepped out of the adjoining elevator shortly after, alone and still adorned in his ceremonial robe.

Bethany had disappeared into the conference room once again. When the door had opened, the Advisor had held Bethany's hand and asked her to visit with him once she was settled. He'd shaken Davis' hand before leaving and said he hoped Davis would come to him with any questions or concerns during his stay.

Bethany waited patiently by the door. As soon as the Advisor stepped into the elevator and the doors closed, she pressed the button for the elevator. He didn't blame her for not wanting to share an elevator. Not a word was spoken until her two friends waylaid her outside the building. At least then some of the tension had eased from her face.

He could guess the gist of the conversation in the conference room. Something along the lines of Aaron demanding her fealty and never-ending obedience. However, if there was something else putting the wounded expression on her face, he needed to get to the bottom of it. He was less sure of Advisor Heyes' approach. Can't believe he was actually sitting here wishing she was a bit chattier.

"You going to tell me about your meetings, or are you going to make me pry it out of you?"

Her gaze met his. "I suppose if I tell you it was nothing that concerned you, you would still feel the need to interrogate me?"

"This feels like an interrogation to you?"

She frowned slightly. "Aaron wanted an accounting of what happened in the States and to express his desire for my support of him ruling the clan. Nothing surprising."

"And do you?"

"Do I what?"

"Support him?"

Bethany fiddled with the edge of her dress. "He is the only one left in line to inherit."

"Doesn't mean he should, and your uncle never designated him as the heir. It opens things up considerably."

"I'm aware, and Advisor Heyes voiced that same opinion as well."

He eased farther back onto the black leather couch and draped an arm over the back. "What else did he have to say?"

"He wants the clan to vote for their new ruler."

"Very democratic of him."

"Yes, I suppose it is. It would appear to be a fairer representation of the wants and needs of the clan."

The cool condensation on the can dripped onto his fingers. He absently wiped it on his jeans and then took a sip. "Appear? You don't think it is?"

"It depends on how the vote is held, doesn't it? And whether all clan members feel safe to vote how they choose and that those votes will be counted accurately."

"True. An unbiased voting process is crucial in order to get results that represent the clan. Did he mention any details about the vote? How it would be done? By whom? When?"

"He wants it held as soon as possible to soothe the

disarray the clan is currently embroiled in. He didn't go into any details about the process however. Aaron has not been supportive of a vote."

"I don't imagine he would be."

"If a vote is held, I'm sure there will be those who would vote for him. He is the traditional choice."

"Is he? I guess that depends on how you look at it. Traditionally the heir must be officially named to follow the rules of succession. If no heir is named, then whoever wants to claim rule has to battle all takers for the right to rule."

Bethany closed her eyes. "I need to get back to my life. I have been away from work too long as it is."

"You're an engineer, right? And design the ships?"

"Essentially, yes. Although there are numerous engineers involved in the process. It's not just me."

"Do you enjoy it?"

She opened her mouth and then closed it with a frown. Took a sip of water and stared at the bottle in her hands. "That's a question with a complicated answer."

"Not really. You either enjoy your job, or you don't."

"Do you? Enjoy your job?"

"Yeah, I do. Security plays to all my strengths, so it suits me just fine."

"I enjoy certain aspects of my job, others not as much. Like I said, the answer is complicated."

The cold fizz of the soda trickled down his throat as he gulped the last of the drink. "What parts don't you like?"

"The bureaucracy can be difficult and frustrating at times. You have to accept the good with the not so good

I suppose."

"Not necessarily. If you don't like something, why can't you change it?"

"It's not that simple. Do you honestly like every aspect of your job?"

"Nope, not all the time, and you can be damn sure I look for a way to get out of it or if it's something I'll have to do again then I find a way to make it more palatable. The point is you don't have to sit back and accept things the way they are if you want them to change, change them."

Bethany gazed out the window as he stared at her profile. Her pale blonde eyebrows pinched together over her dark eyes. She had a way of looking like a fragile porcelain doll, but he knew there was a spine of steel lying beneath the surface.

Chapter Six

"Time to spill, Bethany, and you can begin with that scrumptious Davis." Kate curled her long legs beneath her, leaned back on the sofa, and took a deep sip from her glass of red wine.

"Oh yes, tell us about him! Is he single?" Celeste leaned forward in eager anticipation.

Bethany tucked her hair behind her ear and leaned back against the white wingback chair across from the matching sofa her friends were sitting on. Where Bethany tended to decorate with comfort in mind, Kate preferred a more stylish approach. The chair was attractive to look at, but the texture abraded the back of her legs, and she felt like she was sitting on a hard floor. Right now, she wanted nothing more than to go back to her apartment, climb into bed, and bury her head under the covers for a day or two. She loved her friends dearly but wasn't in the mood to answer any more questions.

"I really don't know much about him." Including whether he was single or not. Did he have a mate waiting at home for him? She squirmed in the chair. It was none of her business or concern if he had someone.

"How long is he staying?"

"I'm not sure about that either. Sorry, I really don't know much."

Celeste pouted and fiddled with her dangly

48

earrings. "Well, poo. I guess I'll have to find out the answers myself. I'll go over and get acquainted. It would be the neighborly thing to do anyway. He's all alone here."

Kate chuckled. "Yes, of course. We must make him feel welcomed. I believe I'll pay him a visit as well."

Bethany frowned and looked away from her friends' gazes. She held her tongue. There was no point. He was a new, attractive man. Nothing would keep them away from him. Besides, Davis was a grown man. He could decide whether he was interested in what they would be offering him or not.

The dull ache behind her eyes started throbbing. She'd watched her friends pursue or be pursued by numerous men over the years of their friendship. Why was it suddenly bothering her when they showed an interest in Davis?

"You've had a time of it, haven't you?" Kate walked over and perched on the arm of Bethany's chair. "Here we are questioning you about the man candy you arrived home with, instead of comforting you after the ordeal you've been through. We're horrible friends."

Bethany smiled wanly up at her friend. "No, you're not. You're the best friends a girl could ever want."

Celeste scooted forward and rested her hand on Bethany's knee. "Did your brother really kill that guy you met at the meet and greet?"

"Celeste!" Kate tossed her empty hand up in the air, jostling her entire body and almost spilling her wine. She swallowed the remainder and rose to place it on a glass side table and sat back down on the arm of the chair.

Celeste gave Kate a wide-eyed stare. "What? You said yourself there are so many rumors flying around, it's hard to know what's true. You said not to believe anything until we talked to Bethany. So that's what I'm doing."

Kate held her hand to her forehead. "That doesn't mean you just hit her with a question like that."

"It's fine, really." Bethany patted Celeste's hand. "Yes, Bryant killed Donald, and he tried to kill me and have me take the blame for Donald's death. He almost succeeded, but thankfully Malcolm Donovan, the leader of the North American clan, made sure to gather all the facts before making a judgement."

She told them all the events which had happened to her while they listened with widened eyes and the occasional horrified gasp. She skimmed over the more graphic details to spare them the images burned into her brain forever.

Kate wrapped her arms around Bethany's shoulders and hugged her. Celeste knelt on the rug, laid her head in Bethany's lap, and sniffled.

Tears filled her eyes. She blinked rapidly and swallowed hard to will them back. If she started crying now, she wasn't sure she would be able to stop.

"To think I thought your brother was cute."

Kate and Bethany shared an exasperated glance and stared down at Celeste's head. Kate shook her head. "You have abysmal taste in men, my dear."

"I know," Celeste whined.

Bethany chuckled. "I am glad to be home. I missed both of you so much. Tell me what's been happening with the two of you while I was gone."

Kate refilled her wine glass, strolled back to the

couch, and sat down. She took a drink of her wine and toyed with the stem of her glass while Celeste jumped up and went in search of a tissue.

"Rumors and suspicion ran rampant throughout the clan. Some said Bryant killed Elsof. Others say it was a plot from the other clans. Another speculation is that Aaron did it." Kate shrugged. "You know how it goes. Everyone has a theory and starts spreading tales like actual facts. The story takes on a life of its own." Kate, a lawyer in the company's legal department, always knew the latest scandal or news.

Celeste sauntered out of the bathroom. "Eddie says that's why we need a new ruler, someone not tainted."

Kate gazed at her over the rim of her glass. "Who is Eddie?"

Celeste frowned and sat down on the couch. "You know who Eddie is. Eddie Heyes."

"Advisor Heyes' son?"

Celeste nodded at Bethany.

"Edward Heyes? Since when do you associate with him? And you call him Eddie?" Kate crossed her legs and rolled her eyes. "What am I saying? Of course, you do."

Celeste wrinkled her nose at Kate. "What's wrong with calling him Eddie? He likes it. We started chatting at the office. He's taken me to lunch a few times. He's worried about his father challenging for rule over the clan. He tried to talk him out of it, but he said his father is adamant about his duty to the clan."

A vague impression of a shorter man with dark hair, a goatee, and glasses formed in Bethany's mind. "He's in human resources, isn't he?"

Celeste tilted her head to the side and frowned.

"Think so, but I'm not really sure."

"If he's in human resources, what's he doing talking to you in accounting?" Kate demanded.

Celeste simply tilted her head and batted her eyelashes at Kate.

Kate rolled her eyes and laughed. "Right, stupid question."

Bethany smiled. Celeste was a personal assistant to the head of the accounting department. Many of the male employees found their way by her desk for one reason or another.

"What's happening in the legal department, Kate? I imagine you have your hands full there, and for that matter the accounting department must be going crazy over the embezzlement allegations."

"Oh, I know. Poor Mr. Deveraux has been having everyone combing over all the files." Bethany grimaced slightly. Mr. Deveraux wasn't known for his tact. She could imagine he had the entire department in a panic. If someone was going to take the fall for not catching Bryant's embezzling, they would all be scrambling to make sure the blame didn't rest with them. How her brother had managed to steal the funds remained a mystery to her as well. He had never been particularly good at math. Had someone in the accounting department helped him, or had it been one more devious misdirect from her brother?

Kate tilted her glass toward Celeste and Bethany. "It's quite the mess. I haven't been assigned the embezzlement case, but between that and the vote Advisor Heyes is calling for, it's all anyone in the office is talking about."

"For the sake of us all it needs to be resolved soon.

We all need a sense of normalcy I think." Bethany pushed to her feet. "Ladies, I really must call it a night. I think I must be a bit jetlagged."

Celeste and Kate both stood and gave her a kiss on the cheek and a hug.

Kate escorted her to the door. "How about we plan a get together for later in the week once you've recovered a bit?"

Bethany nodded her assent and walked to the elevator. Kate's door shut behind her with a soft click. She rubbed at the painful drumming between her eyes. The elevator pinged its arrival, and the doors slid open to a thankfully empty compartment. Leaning her head against the cold steel wall, she sighed.

An alarm startled her. She stared at the instrument panel and realized she hadn't pushed a button for the floor.

Her finger hesitated over the larger lobby button before lifting and pressing the smooth round one to go up to the top floor—her brother's floor.

This building, one of the newest residential buildings on the compound, offered more spacious and luxurious accommodations to those who could afford the expense. It had been built at the same time as the office building it stood beside. Everyone in the clan who resided on the compound had been on high alert while the construction crews had been on sight. She had been just a child at the time, but she had heard many tales. One in particular had always amused her and stuck in her mind. One of the construction crew members had spotted a lion and started shouting about a loose zoo animal. Of course, it had been a Risharden shifting, completely unaware she was in full view from the tall building. The clan had been able to hush it up, but allowing any non-Risharden on the compound was a rare occurrence. They put ample effort to ensure clan members were trained in any skills which might be needed on the compound, so they wouldn't accidently expose the clan's secrets to outsiders.

The doors opened, but she hesitated. She should push the button for the lobby and leave, but instead she stepped out and looked right and left. No one was about. She padded down the carpeted hallway to her brother's door. Half expecting to see signs declaring a murderous traitor once lived here or at the very least caution tape spread across the opening, she stared at the bare door. It looked completely normal.

She had no key, no way to get inside. What could she possibly hope to find anyway? It's not like she had been invited over often. She'd only been there perhaps a half a dozen times over the years. There were probably no mementos waiting for her to collect. And why would she want anything of his anyway? He'd tried to kill her. He'd felt no brotherly love for her at all, obviously. She had been simply a tool for him to use.

A tear spilled over, and she swiped the back of her hand across her cheek. Why was she standing here crying like a little fool? She sniffed and blinked back the tears.

She was here. She might as well try the door. She almost jumped when the handle rotated easily in her hand.

Peeking inside, she sucked in a breath. It looked the same. His modern furniture was still there. Why did she think it would be empty? Who would have taken care of the details? It probably fell to her to deal with. She was his closest relative after all.

Hesitantly stepping over the threshold, she gazed around the shadowed interior trying to recall where a light switch was located. A sound to her right, from the direction of her brother's bedroom, almost made her call out to see if someone was there, but she froze.

Who would be here? At this time of day? With no lights on?

Bethany spun around and grasped the door handle. She was leaving. She would return with a guard. Perhaps she was letting paranoia get the best of her, but it was better to look stupid than actually be stupid.

A feeling of dread washed over her.

She truly wasn't alone.

The ominous sound of rapid footfalls and the brush of fabric sent panic racing through her system. She grappled with the handle, but it slipped through her sweaty palms.

A rush of movement disturbed the air behind her. Before she could turn to face the intruder, she was shoved into the door.

Her head bounced against the solid metal door.

The coppery taste of blood filled her mouth.

She threw out her hands to find purchase.

Pain exploded in the back of her head.

Weakness dragged her down. Darkness crept across her vision and painted it black.

Chapter Seven

The heavy stairwell door opened silently. He hesitated a moment before entering the hallway. The scent enveloping Davis caused him to jerk his head up. He knew that scent—he'd chased it for weeks.

Bethany had been here recently.

Why? Her friends' apartment was in this building, but not on this floor. The only reason he could think of for her to be here was her brother's apartment. But the question was why?

Davis strode down the hallway intending to confront her and find out the reason.

As he neared the door, a smell assaulted his senses.

Blood.

The instinct to rush the door surged through him, but he pushed the feeling down. He needed to be cautious before he barreled inside into the unknown and possibly endangered her even more. He paused to listen and draw the scents in deeper to analyze them. Hers wasn't the only scent, there were others, but not as recent.

Silence from the apartment propelled him forward. He grasped the handle. It spun easily in his hand.

One look at her body on the floor sent a white-hot rage spiraling through him.

After a quick glance around, he shut the door and dropped to his knees beside her.

Her chest rose and fell with each breath. His fingers searched and found her pulse strong and steady.

Davis regretfully stood and briskly walked through the apartment. He'd been here before and remembered the layout. After confirming visually they were alone, he rushed back to Bethany.

"Bethany?" He scanned her from head to toe, looking for injuries. The only wound he could see to account for the scent of blood was a split lip. He gently probed the back of her head.

His fingers grazed a small lump. Bethany moaned and angled her head away from his touch. Her eyes fluttered open, and she raised her hand to her head, wincing at the movement.

"Easy."

Her gaze sought his. "Davis? What happened…?"

She surged up, only to fall back and groan in pain.

"Take it easy."

"Someone was here." She rested her frame on her elbows and searched frantically behind her.

"It's all right. They're gone."

Davis stood and leaned down to tentatively lift her up in his arms. He didn't want to add to her pain. Anger choked him. He wanted to hunt down whoever did this to her, but first he needed to see the extent of her injuries and ensure her safety.

"What are you doing? I am fine. Put me down."

He ignored her order and carried her to the couch and set her down gingerly. She winced as she shifted and started to sit up.

"Lie still."

"I told you, I am fine. The pain is already beginning to lessen. You know we heal quickly."

Davis frowned and sat on the coffee table next to her. "Tell me what happened."

Bethany grimaced when her fingers probed the sore spot on the back of her head. She rotated her neck to loosen her stiffened muscles. "I told you, someone was here. They shoved me into the door, and then hit me in the back of the head with something."

His fists clenched at his side.

"What were you doing here?"

Sighing, she smoothed her dress over her legs. "I'm not really sure. I left Kate's, and I found myself wandering up here." She shrugged and then stiffened. Whoever pushed her had left a mark. She closed her eyes briefly to avoid his hard stare and then looked around her brother's flat before meeting Davis' gaze once again.

"What are *you* doing here?"

He returned her gaze steadily. "I wanted to have a look around. See if anything had changed since I was here last. Besides, you know there are still questions to be answered about your brother and the things he did, especially confirming whether he did them alone."

"Has it changed?"

Shrugging he stood and glanced around. "Not much that I can see. I only had a cursory look to make sure no one remained here." He walked over to flick the light switch on the wall on. "Take me through it step by step. You left Kate's apartment…"

He wandered around the room and in and out of the guest room, glancing over his shoulder at her.

Rubbing the soft cotton material of her dress between her fingertips, she retraced her steps out loud for Davis. "I was in the elevator, and I decided to come up here. I'm not really sure why, or what I expected. The door was unlocked so I walked in. I thought maybe it had been emptied already, but that really doesn't make any sense. I am his sister, so that is my responsibility. I was looking for a light switch when I thought I heard something from Bryant's bedroom. It startled me, and I decided to leave and go get a guard."

She swallowed and stared at the floor. "Before I could, I felt someone behind me. They shoved me into the door and hit me. The next thing I remember was waking up to see you hovering over me."

Pushing up from the couch, she stood. The room wavered slightly, but she stiffened her spine and rode it out. Davis strode over to stand in front of her. He tilted her chin to stare into her eyes. She froze at the warmth of his hand on her chilled skin. His hazel gaze searched her features. The breath stuttered in her chest. A warmth spread through her.

"Where is your clan healer? You need to be checked out."

Bethany pulled her head back from his grasp and twisted away. "I am fine. I certainly do not need the healer." She wrapped her arms around her waist. "We should contact the guards. Whoever it was, is probably a thief. I have no idea how to determine what they might have stolen, but security needs to be informed."

"Yeah, maybe. You call the guards. I'm going to take another look around your brother's room and lab."

"Fine. You are more likely to notice something missing than I would. I haven't been here in at least two years."

His gaze tracked her as she walked to the phone and called the security desk and reported the break in.

Davis disappeared into Bryant's bedroom. She hung up the phone and walked stiffly down the hallway into his room.

The sight of the hidden lab caused bile to churn in her stomach.

How could she have not known her brother at all?

The blood drained from her face as she stood in the doorway gazing around at her brother's perfidy.

"That's it. If you won't go to the healer, you're at least going to rest. The last thing I need is you passing out and the guards arriving." He strode toward her intending to carry her back to the couch. He thought about the bed behind her, but it seemed wrong somehow, and he didn't think she would feel any better there.

She held up a hand and turned away when the front door opened, and people entered the apartment. It made him realize once again how much of a sitting duck she had been entering the apartment alone.

"Wait." He grasped her arm to halt her progress and then stepped in front of her as two guards entered the bedroom.

She peeked around his arm and wanly smiled at the guards.

The guards glared at him. The larger of the two stepped forward. "Lady Bethany, are you hurt?"

"She was attacked—what do you think?"

"I'm fine. Just a bump on the head. I don't know what they were doing here or what they were looking for, but I wanted security to be aware of the intrusion."

The guard gazed about the room before focusing his attention back on them. "You think someone wanted to steal his stuff?" He glared at Davis. "Where were you when she was attacked?"

Davis folded his arms over his chest and rocked back on his heels. Behind him, Bethany sucked in a breath.

"I was alone. Well, except for whoever hit me. Mr. Campbell found me. I suppose whoever it was could have been here to steal something, but I don't know what."

The guards' gazes flicked back and forth between the two of them. He could practically see their minds working. It wouldn't be long before they pinned the attack on him.

"Did you notice anything familiar about your attacker, Lady Bethany?"

"No, they hit me from behind. I didn't see anything."

"Perhaps you had an impression of their size? Were they much taller than you?"

Davis refrained from rolling his eyes and simply waited silently. He supposed it was a small point in his favor Bethany hadn't jumped to the same conclusion the guard had and started pointing her delicate little finger at him. "I…I'm sorry, but no. I really couldn't say."

"What were you doing here, Mr. Campbell? If you weren't with Lady Bethany, how is it you arrived at the flat just as she was being attacked?"

"I arrived after her attack. If I had arrived during, then I could have prevented it, or at the very least captured her attacker. As to the why, I'm here on council authority. Feel free to question their reasons."

The guards glanced down and away.

Bethany stepped out from behind him. "I think it

might be prudent to post a guard outside my brother's door until it can be determined there is nothing dangerous remaining in his lab or any evidence of his crimes. Please also be sure to inform my cousin and Advisor Heyes of the incident. Although I'm certain it was a simple break-in, they will want to be apprised of the situation in case it concerns the ongoing investigation of my brother's crimes."

"Of course, Lady Bethany."

"Thank you. I am tired and want to return to my flat. If there are any further questions for me, please contact me tomorrow. Mr. Campbell, would you please accompany me?"

Bethany started for the door. The guards parted for her, giving her a slight bow as she passed.

Davis dropped his hands to his sides and slowly ambled behind her. She kept a brisk pace out of the apartment and down the hall to the elevator. He stayed abreast of her once she exited the apartment to keep a watchful eye out.

After they entered the elevator, she pushed the button for the lobby and faced him. "Care to tell me what you were doing in the apartment?"

"As I told the guards, council business."

A smirk inched across his face. The urge to stamp her foot came and went. The guards were less than subtle about their accusation Davis was responsible for her ambush and the break- in of Bryant's flat.

Bethany supposed it was possible. She would be a fool not to consider that possibility. Davis had been the only one there when she woke up. It was a bit convenient.

However, she had no feeling of malicious intent

around him. Wouldn't she feel some fear? Sense in some way if he was the one who attacked her?

Her faith in her instincts had grown a bit tarnished of late, but she couldn't believe Davis was capable of attacking her.

Davis sighed. "I told you earlier, I wanted to investigate your brother's apartment to see if anything had changed. I didn't attack you, Bethany."

She held his gaze. "I didn't think you did."

He nodded. "Think back over the incident again. Did you notice anything at all about who attacked you?"

Bethany rubbed her forehead. The drumming pain had transformed into a steady stream of agony. Even though her kind healed remarkably fast from injury, she was still prone to migraines. The stress of her life was catching up to her.

"No. I heard the sound, panicked, and tried to flee. I heard a rustle behind me and then felt the shove, and the blow on my head."

"A rustle? You didn't mention that before. What kind of rustle?"

The elevator doors opened, and they walked in silence out of the building. Bethany stopped on the sidewalk. "A rustle of clothing. A jacket. The sound it makes when the material rubs together."

"Okay, that's something. Perhaps if there's any video footage of the building it will give us something to search for. I didn't notice any surveillance cameras except in the lobby. Anything else? A smell?"

Bethany slowly shook her head. Cameras hadn't occurred to her. Surely something should have been captured. "My sense of smell is poor even by human

63

standards I'm afraid."

"Mine's not."

She stared up at him.

"Bethany, the only scent I detected was yours. No other scent existed. It wasn't a simple break-in."

Chapter Eight

The patter of rain against her bedroom window prodded Bethany out of her reverie. Davis said there had been no other scent but hers. Someone had used Bryant's scent blocker. Had they been in his apartment looking for more? Had they stolen it previously? Had her brother given it to them? Had they been working with him? For him? Or had he been working for them?

So many thoughts and questions raced through her mind.

Bethany gently shook her head.

Focus, Bethany. Musing over her brother and who he may or may not have been working with would not solve her biggest dilemma at the moment.

Davis was waiting in her living room, refusing to leave.

Which meant he would be sleeping in her flat a few steps away from her bedroom. Her cozy flat shrank before her eyes.

He'd insisted she wasn't safe, and no amount of convincing him to the contrary had worked when they'd arrived back at her flat. She'd finally given up trying and muttered to him about getting bedding for the couch.

She glanced down at the pillow and wool, plaid blanket she'd pulled down from the top of her closet. Placing them on her bed, she raised up on her tippy toes to grab a set of forest green sheets and a matching pillowcase as well.

The soft rain had increased to a staccato of beats against the window. Good. The sound of rain had always helped her to sleep. She had a feeling she would need all the help she could get tonight.

The soft bedding filled and overflowed her arms as she trudged out of her bedroom and into the living room. Davis stood staring out the window. He glanced over his shoulder at her, and then walked over to take the pile from her arms.

His warm hands brushed against hers—sending a tingle of awareness racing up her arms. She snatched her hands away and clasped them together behind her back.

He dropped the bedding on the open sofa bed. He must have opened it while she was in the bedroom. She glanced around the room to see he had tucked her table against the wall and pushed back the other furniture to make room.

Davis began pulling the sheet across the mattress. Bethany quickly stepped forward to grasp the other side and help him.

"I don't suppose there is any point in trying again to make you listen to reason about this?"

"Nope."

"You would be much more comfortable in your suite." Bethany glanced down the length of the mattress. "I doubt you will even fit on this."

"It's fine. I've slept on worse."

They also fixed the top sheet and the blanket together. "Even if it wasn't a simple break-in, the odds that whoever it was would come after me have to be astronomical. Why would they? If they wanted to hurt me, they had the opportunity while I was unconscious."

A slight shudder rippled over her skin as visions of what could have happened to her played in her head.

Davis stiffened and spoke through a clenched jaw. "Has it not occurred to you that something spooked them before they could kill you? Your brother had a hidden lab in his apartment. It's not out of the realm of possibility he also had a hidden exit that no one has discovered yet. Or your attacker simply walked out the front door before I arrived. The scent blocker masked any smell I could have gotten to track them. They still may come after you to finish the job."

Bethany dropped her gaze and wrapped her arms about her waist.

"I think it makes more sense that I surprised them by entering the apartment, and they simply wanted out and I blocked their escape."

"Your Pollyanna attitude is going to get you killed."

"I hardly think being realistic and logical can be construed as a Pollyanna attitude. You naturally see the danger in every situation and react accordingly. I am sure that makes you good at your job. I just do not see the point in overreacting."

Davis stalked around the bed toward her. Determination etched in his features and stance.

Bethany dropped her arms and took a small step back before she caught herself and stood her ground. She would not be intimidated by him, or anyone, ever again.

He stopped inches from her, looming over her. She raised her chin and met his gaze.

"Overreacting? How's this for overreacting?"

He snatched her against him, wrapping his arms around her.

She gasped and slapped her hands flat against his chest.

Blinking up at him, she opened her mouth to disabuse him of the notion scare tactics would work with her.

His head dipped down, and his lips captured hers before she could utter a word.

Her mind went blank—every thought fluttering right out of her head.

Soft lips, warm breath, and a tight embrace consumed her thoughts.

Stunned pleasure heated her skin.

His tongue sought entrance, and she granted it welcomingly.

The dark, exotic taste of him exploded in her mouth.

Her fingers clenched his shirt in her fists. She rose on her tippy toes to have more access.

Firm hands grasped her hips.

Suddenly, he wrenched his mouth away from hers and lifted and set her back from him.

Bethany leaned forward slightly, not ready to give up the pleasure of his embrace.

Davis spun away and stalked to the window, again staring out into the dark, rainy night.

Comprehension dawned, and a chill spread over her sensitized skin.

He rolled his shoulders and cracked his neck.

Shame and embarrassment hunched *her* shoulders. Her overenthusiastic response to his kiss had not been well received. What had he expected from her? A slap in the face? Had he been trying to teach her lesson? Show her how vulnerable she was?

Bethany clasped her hands together. She was hardly overly experienced in the area of desire, but she didn't think he had been unaffected by their kiss. His plan may have backfired on him.

She started to turn toward her bedroom but halted the movement.

Avoiding confrontation had always been her pattern, but she'd promised herself she wasn't going to run and hide anymore. She was an owl, not an ostrich.

"Why did you kiss me?"

His back stiffened.

"Why do you think?"

"That isn't an answer. It's irrelevant what I think. I would like to know why please."

He cocked his head slightly, so she could see his reflection in the glass. "To prove a point."

Bethany nodded and glanced down at the honey gold planks of the wood floor. It was as she thought. Davis believed her to be weak and unable to defend herself. Their brief history together had hardly shown him differently. She had been duped, betrayed, and left for dead by her own brother.

"I am not weak." She wasn't entirely sure whether she was telling him or herself, but she needed to say the words.

Davis faced her and frowned.

Before he could speak and possibly list all the reasons why he thought she was, Bethany clenched her fists at her sides and plowed on, determined to prove her statement to herself and him. "I am not weak. I realize recent events may have portrayed me in a poor light, but I survived. That makes me strong, not weak."

"I agree."

Surprised, Bethany met his gaze.

"I don't think you're weak. I never did. You're a survivor. Most wouldn't have endured what you have."

She searched his features and words for any hint of sarcasm but found none. "Oh. Well, then."

"However, that doesn't mean you don't need protection."

Bethany shifted and sighed.

"You're not a fighter. Have you ever been trained in how to defend yourself?"

"No, it was frowned upon." She had asked her uncle once if she could take some fighting classes. He had laughed at her and said it was both unnecessary and beneath her station. "I don't know if you noticed, but there are only two female guards here."

"I noticed."

Of course, he did. He noticed everything.

"They had to battle their way to their positions. They are the first. My uncle had male chauvinistic tendencies."

"No kidding." Davis sighed and propped his hands on his hips. "Look, if you want, I will show you some basic moves."

"Yes, please." Bethany stepped forward.

He held up his hand. "Not tonight. We can start tomorrow. It's been a long day, and you should get some rest."

She tried not to let her disappointment show. She wanted to learn. She never wanted to feel vulnerable again.

Bethany turned to go after whispering, "Goodnight."

Davis mumbled, "Night" in response and rubbed his hands over his face as soon as the door closed behind her.

Holy shit!

The woman nearly brought him to his knees.

His body was on fire with need. Luckily, she was too naïve to notice. Touching her had been a colossal mistake.

She thought the point he had been trying to prove was that she was vulnerable and needed protection, and maybe it had been his initial intent. But somewhere between his first steps and when he reached her and stood staring down at her upturned face, it had changed to proving to himself he didn't want her. He didn't crave the touch of her soft skin, or her slight body beneath his hands. She wasn't his mate.

No way. How could she be? Davis plopped down on the edge of the mattress and rubbed his face roughly with the palms of his hands. Yeah, keep arguing with yourself, Davis.

She was his.

And now what the hell was he going to do?

Chapter Nine

Despite listening to the soft pitter-patter of rain, Bethany found herself lying in bed, wide awake and staring at the swirling pattern of paint on the ceiling. She snuggled deeper into her soft mattress, tugging the baby blue duvet and crisp white sheets up to her chin. A slight, fresh, floral scent rose from the sheets. She breathed deeply and closed her eyes, only to pop them open a moment later.

She could hear him shifting on the sofa bed in the living room. If she could hear him, it stood to reason he would hear any movement she made.

Her fingers clenched over the sheet and pulled it up to the tip of her nose. Holding still as a statue, she listened for any more sounds emanating from the other room. Perhaps if he started to snore she would relax enough to find some sleep.

Having a man lying a thin wall away from her was a novel experience. A man she found extraordinarily attractive and who had just kissed her senseless. She'd been unconscious or too ill and in shock to care about the lack of privacy when she'd been held prisoner by the North American clan.

To prove a point.

Rolling her eyes, she turned on her side and pulled her knees up to her chest and wrapped her arms around her feather pillow.

She had no business fixating on his kiss, or even kissing him in the first place. The last time she allowed herself to feel a romantic interest in a man he had ended up murdered, and she'd almost lost her life as well.

Donald had been sweet and gentle. He hadn't deserved his fate. He'd lost his life because the two of them had found some comfort in one another, both knowing their search for a mate had been a waste of time.

Poor Donald. He wanted nothing more than to find his mate and start a family. Now the dream was forever lost. Because of her.

One decision changed his destiny.

If he had chosen someone else to spend time with, or had simply gone home, he would still be alive. If she had gone home, he would be alive.

A tear trailed down the length of her nose, and she absently wiped it away.

Why had she ever gone to the meet and greet?

It was out of character. She should have stayed on her path. Instead, she had let Celeste and Kate talk her into going. They had dared her, teased she would never go through with it. She had been in a rut, feeling aimless and a bit lonely. So, of course, she had to prove them wrong.

So foolish, and Donald had paid the price.

Wiping her wet cheeks on her pillow, she hugged it closer. Only the soft beats of rain from outside could be heard.

Her eyelids slid down, shuttering out the night, and her mind drifted into dreamland.

She ran down a dark alley. The sound of her footsteps hitting the stones echoed back to her. The splash of a puddle soaked her foot and splattered her ankle. Fear and panic squeezed at her chest. Her breaths sawed from her lungs. There, what was that? The flap of enormous wings hovered above her. She gasped in horror.

Bethany jerked awake. Her palms were flat against the bed. The bedding shoved to the bottom of the bed. Her ivory nightgown was twisted around her hips and upper thighs. Her chest rapidly rose and fell. Harsh gulps of air filled her ears. Gazing about the darkened room, she searched every corner and shadow. Fear held her immobile.

The door to her bedroom swung open, and a figure loomed in the opening.

She sucked in a panicked breath, and her gaze darted right and left looking for an escape.

"Are you all right? What happened?"

Davis. It was Davis. The sight of his familiar form calmed her racing heart. She inhaled deeply and slowly, and then pulled herself to a seated position while yanking her nightgown down to cover her legs.

His gaze searched the room before once again landing on her.

"I had a nightmare. It's nothing. I'm sorry for disturbing your sleep." Her voice sounded harsh to her ears. Her throat was dry and achy.

Stepping farther into her room, the privy light she had left on cast a glow around him. His chest was bare, and his jeans unsnapped. He must have hastily pulled them on. Had she screamed?

"Do you want to talk about it?"

She blinked at him and then looked away. "Um, no, but thank you. It was just a silly dream." She stared at the rumpled bedding at the foot of her bed.

"You've been through a lot lately. I'd be more surprised if you didn't have nightmares."

Tears pricked the back of her eyes. She dragged the pillow into her lap and hugged it to her chest.

"Would you like some water?"

She gave him a tight nod and peeked up at him through her damp lashes. He turned and strode into the kitchen. From the bed she had a clear view. Bethany watched him turn on the light above the stove before opening her cabinets to find a glass.

Heaving a deep sigh, she glanced around her room. Fear rose as she searched all the lengthy shadows. She would be sleeping with a light on for the rest of the night.

Davis returned from the kitchen and handed her a glass of water.

She smiled and whispered, "Thank you," before taking a drink. She reached to place the glass on her nightstand, but he took it from her hand and placed it there himself.

He bent and grasped her bedding, pulling it up over the bed to cover her. She stared at the top of his head as he reached across her to tuck it around her. She couldn't recall a single instance of anyone ever tucking her in bed, not even as a child.

Glancing at her briefly, he stepped back from the bed. "Can I get you anything else? Anything I can do for you?"

"No, thank you. I'll be fine."

He absently nodded and looked around the room.

"Goodnight, Davis."

"'Night."

As soon as he stepped out of the room, closing the door behind him, she lunged across the bed and snapped on the light on her nightstand. Staring at the door, she listened for his return. He was sure to notice the light, but would he understand her need not to be left in the dark, or would he think something was wrong?

The creak of the sofa bed brought a sigh of relief.

She leaned back against the fabric of her headboard and pulled the bedding back over her body. It was doubtful she would get any more sleep tonight.

****

"What's your schedule for today?" She flitted about the tiny kitchen making tea. She hadn't spoken to him this morning except for a quick *good morning* when she had emerged from her bedroom.

She had yet to look at him, either.

Bethany paused a moment with her back to him, and then continued to pour herself a cup of tea. He admired the way her black leggings hugged every curve before disappearing under a purple top. His gaze lingered over the shape of her ass, which was revealed to him each time she stretched to reach into the cabinet over her head.

"I don't have anything scheduled. Technically, I'm still on holiday, so I don't report to work until next week."

Bethany turned around, glanced in his direction briefly, and leaned against the counter sipping her tea.

"Good. That makes it easier."

"Makes what easier?"

"Protecting you."

"For how long? I want to know the amount of time

you have appointed yourself my bodyguard for. This cannot continue indefinitely, so what is the time limit? You certainly cannot follow me to my job at the company. There are security issues involved. You do not have the proper clearance to be in my department. Besides, you are here to report to the council—not be my personal bodyguard. I hardly think Malcolm Donovan would approve."

Bethany straightened and set her cup down on the counter. "In fact, perhaps we should give him a call and get his perspective on the situation. I am sure he could make you see reason."

"Be my guest." Davis walked over to the kitchen and held out his cell phone to her. She glanced at the phone and then up to his face. He leaned toward her. "I should mention that I spoke to him already this morning while you were in the shower."

One pale blonde eyebrow arched. "And?"

"Something you should know about Malcolm is he takes his responsibilities seriously."

"I never doubted he did, but I am not one of his responsibilities."

"Ah, but see, that's where you're wrong. Ever since you were a guest of our clan, he extended his protection to you. It didn't end simply because you left."

"As admirable as that is, I am not part of his clan. He has no obligation to me, nor is any needed. I am not in danger."

He shrugged. "Feel free to argue with him. Although, it's not an approach I would recommend. He doesn't care to be questioned over his decisions."

Bethany walked out of the kitchen area. "You

didn't answer how long."

"For as long as I believe you're in danger."

She whirled back to face him. "That's unacceptable. There needs to be a time frame. If there are no further attempts on my life in the next day…two at the most, then you must consent to end this."

Davis folded his arms across his chest and leaned back against the counter. He fought the urge to smile. With her blonde cap of hair swirling about her face, she looked like an angry sprite. He didn't think she would appreciate the analogy though.

"How about this? I will agree to revisit the conversation."

Bethany wanted to continue discussing the matter, but instead she gave him a reluctant nod. He wasn't going to back down, and there was no point in arguing any further. However, if he didn't become more reasonable when nothing else happened, she would be the one calling Malcolm Donovan. Facing that giant was preferable to enduring more restless nights and Davis following her every move. She couldn't handle the stress and frustration.

"How about we work on some of those self-defense moves I promised you?"

She glanced at him beneath her lashes. "Do I get to hit you?"

A slow smile spread across his face. "You can try."

Chapter Ten

"The number one rule to remember is do not engage unless you have no other options. Hide, run, get help first, or in your case, fly. If none of those options are available, then, and only then, do you confront your attacker. Understood?"

"Trust me, I have no wish to fight anyone. But I would like to know how to defend myself if I'm ever in a dangerous predicament again."

Davis placed the gray-tufted ottoman on the matching chair and picked both up with ease. He placed them against the wall with the other furniture already positioned there out of the way. "Watch their eyes. People often telegraph their intention before they make a movement. If their gaze focuses on a certain area, get ready to defend yourself."

Bethany nodded and knelt to roll up her lavender area rug. Davis scooped it up and dropped it on the couch. Her living space was small, and even with everything shoved against the walls there wasn't much space to maneuver. She hoped he wasn't planning on anything too acrobatic. She didn't want to alarm her neighbors with the sounds of fighting or breaking furniture. Not only could she not afford to replace any damaged pieces, but she didn't relish the thought of anyone knowing Davis was attempting to teach her self-defense. Or the fact he was temporarily staying with her. Of course, if she didn't convince him to abandon the idea she was in danger and in need of his protection soon, then her neighbors would begin to suspect something was going on when he followed her around everywhere and didn't leave to go back to his suite.

"Are you listening?"

Davis stood with his hands on his hips, facing her. She gave him an absent nod. "Of course, you said to watch their eyes."

"Then why are you staring at the floor instead of watching my eyes?"

Bethany blinked and shot her gaze up to collide with his own. His hazel eyes were pinned on her. Did he plan to rush her with no instruction? What did he expect her to do? He was twice her size and could no doubt squash her like a bug. "Sorry. I didn't realize you were starting."

"Any opponent you may have will not wait for you to get prepared. You need to be on guard and watchful. Observe your surroundings at all times and be ready."

She nodded, straightened her shoulders, and widened her stance slightly all the while keeping her gaze on his.

"Not only are the eyes important to give an idea of any move they're planning, but it's also a vulnerable spot on the body. Along with the throat." Davis stepped toward her, and Bethany leaped back. "Relax. I just want to show you." He took her hand in his and turned it over. "Use the heel of your hand." He traced a finger over her palm and along the edge. A shiver danced over her skin. She shook it off and focused on his words.

"Using the heel of your hand to strike at the eyes, throat, or nose will cause damage to your attacker while making it less likely to incur injury to your hand." He gently folded over her fingers and pulled her hand toward him to demonstrate hitting the vulnerable spots on his head.

Davis loosely clasped her wrist as he directed her hand to each target on his head. His eyelashes brushed against her palm. Her thumb trailed down the length of his nose as he repositioned her hand. He held her hand against his throat as he swallowed hard.

"Your objective is to do some quick damage to incapacitate your attacker, so you can escape." The vibration of his words and heat of his skin pulsed against her hand.

He released her, and she clenched her hand against her abdomen. "Put the strength of your entire body behind your movements and follow through. After the face, go for the groin."

Her gaze involuntarily dropped to the zipper of his black jeans before she snapped it back to his face and swallowed hard. "You're assuming my attacker is a man. Although I suppose it is a more likely scenario for an attacker to be male, women are capable of violence as well."

"The groin is a vulnerable area on the body for both a man and woman." Davis clasped her hip, and the breath stuttered in her chest. His hand trailed down the outside of her thigh. She had worn leggings thinking them an appropriate choice for ease of movement. It had never occurred to her the thin layer of material would provide little barrier to the heat and strength of his hands on her body.

"If you're farther away, use your foot." He placed his hand behind her knee, and lifted her leg. Her gaze remained trapped by his. "Up close, like this, use your knee." He pressed her knee lightly against his groin.

Bethany licked her lips, and his gaze dropped to track the movement of her tongue. He swelled against her knee, and she couldn't help but lean a little closer as her gaze trailed down the white T-shirt stretched tightly across his chest and over his flat abdomen. His erection strained at his zipper, and Bethany bit her lip.

Davis pulled her leg over his hip and wrapped his other arm around her back, lifting Bethany against him. She grabbed onto his shoulders as he lowered them both to the floor. Her startled gaze collided with his.

"If the assailant gets you to the floor, try to use both your feet to throw them off. If you don't have the space, use your hips." She listened to the rumble of his voice above her, as his hand released her leg and grasped her hip and pulled her lower half tight against his body. He leaned over her, supported by his elbow. His handsome face hovered mere inches above Bethany's own.

"Do whatever you can and use whatever you have to fight back. Smash his or her nose with the top of your head and then hit, kick, and buck to get them off of you. Understood?"

Her chest rose and fell with labored breaths. She couldn't take her gaze off his hazel eyes.

"Bethany?"

"Mmhmm."

"Good." He rolled off her and sprang to his feet.

She dropped her now empty hands to the floor and stared at the ceiling.

Davis spun away from her and rubbed the back of his neck. He dropped his arm and stalked over to the kitchen area to grab a glass of ice water. He didn't dare glance at Bethany still lying on the floor.

The chilled water soothed his parched throat but did nothing to put out the fire raging in his body. It had taken everything he had to pull away from her tempting little body cradling his. He was rock hard and aching for her.

How the hell was he supposed to keep his head on straight when a simple touch from her burned him alive? He tilted his head back and guzzled the remaining water in his glass. Teaching Bethany self-defense may very well be the death of him.

Chapter Eleven

At the soft knock on her front door, Bethany lunged to her feet. She tiptoed to her bedroom door and listened closely as Davis walked across her living area to answer the door. After scrambling off the floor this morning and telling Davis she had had enough training for the day, she returned to her room and started pacing the floor. Once it had occurred to her he could hear her pacing, she had promptly dropped down on the bed to sit and brood over her embarrassing fascination with her self-appointed bodyguard. The knock on the door signaled a welcome reprieve from the turmoil of her own thoughts. She couldn't continue to hide in her bedroom, but she hadn't drummed up enough courage to face him either.

The soft diction of his greeting when Davis opened the door to her flat identified her visitor as Advisor Heyes. Smoothing her top, she opened her door and stepped over the threshold. Advisor Heyes met her gaze and smiled while Davis continued to glower.

"Good afternoon, Advisor Heyes. What can I do for you?"

"Ah, Lady Bethany, I received word about your ordeal, and I wanted to check on your wellbeing."

"That's very kind of you, but as you can see I am fine."

"How did you hear about it?"

Bethany glanced at Davis when he asked the question and then returned her attention to Advisor Heyes. She assumed one of the guards had informed him, but she understood the need to be certain.

"One of the guards reported the incident to me. He is loyal to the clan as well as Lady Bethany and felt it his duty to inform me of the break-in and her assault."

Davis folded his arms across his chest and stared at the advisor. "By loyal to the clan do you mean loyal to you? The guard is one of your supporters?"

Bethany opened her mouth to intercede, but promptly snapped it closed. She wanted to hear the answer.

"I meant what I said. He is loyal to the clan and wants what is best for the clan, as do I. He has bestowed on me his endorsement to rule. I have made no secret of my intentions, Mr. Campbell."

She stepped forward to ease the growing tension. "I am certain Davis meant no offense." From the corner of her eye, she saw Davis turning his head toward her. Bethany didn't have to look at him to know the sarcastic slant of his eyebrow would be arched over his skeptic glare. She smiled at the advisor and hoped he would keep his attention focused on her and Davis would not feel the need to interrupt and contradict her. "I appreciate your concern, but I am unharmed. My concern lies with the fact someone broke into my brother's apartment."

Advisor Heyes gently took her hand and sandwiched it between his two. "Have no fear. I took no offense at your staunch defender's questions. It is admirable he takes his duty to protect you so seriously. I too am deeply concerned one of our own trespassed and attacked you. You have my assurance the matter will be given the utmost attention it deserves. If you feel up to it, I would like to inquire what you believe the intruder had been doing inside the apartment?"

"I cannot be sure, of course, but…"

"How can she possibly speculate? You're asking her to guess about an unknown assailant's motives. Who knows why someone was in there? It could have been a simple curiosity seeker who panicked at her entry. Or do you think you have another criminal hiding in your midst?"

Bethany stared up at Davis and wondered what game he was playing. He obviously didn't want her talking about their theory that Bryant might have an accomplice.

"What may I ask were you doing there, Mr. Campbell? The guard said it was you who found Lady Bethany. You did not accompany her?"

"No, he didn't. I decided on a whim to go there. Luckily for me, Davis appeared when he did."

The advisor patted her hand and released it. "Yes, of course. Well, I will be on my way. I am glad to see you are well. Until the situation is resolved perhaps it is best if you refrain from visiting your brother's quarters again. I would not like to see anything bad happen to you."

"Is that a threat?" Davis dropped his arms and scowled at the man.

"Certainly not! I was expressing my concern for her safety."

Bethany sidled between them. "Thank you, and please let me know if you do hear anything. I would like to resolve the matter of my brother's belongings and put it all behind me. You do understand?"

"Yes, I do, and if at any time you would like to speak to me in confidence about your brother, or anything for that matter... Please know my door is always open to you. I am still the clan's spiritual advisor, and I am available to provide counsel or a friendly ear."

She smiled and opened the door. "That is very kind of you. I will keep it in mind."

He nodded and, after a quick glance at Davis, exited the flat. Bethany closed the door and leaned against the warm wood with a sigh. The heat of Davis' stare called to her, but she refused to acknowledge him. Why was he constantly antagonizing everyone around him?

Davis' hand brushed her side when he leaned forward and locked the door. Her gaze shot up to his as he leaned toward her. There was a telltale click of the deadbolt as he flicked it closed as well. His gaze remained locked on hers as he straightened.

Bethany licked her lips and stepped past him into the kitchen area to pour herself a glass of water.

"Do you care to tell me why you didn't want me mentioning the possibility Bryant had an accomplice? You cannot possibly suspect Advisor Heyes."

Davis walked over and leaned against the counter with his arms and ankles crossed. Her small kitchen resembled a child's play kitchen with him standing in the middle. "I suspect everyone until they can be cleared completely. There's no point in advertising our knowledge that whoever attacked you must be using your brother's scent blocker. You might as well put a neon sign over your head declaring you're a threat that needs to be taken out."

"Fine, but aren't we hampering any investigation by not giving them all the facts?"

"No offense, sweetheart, but I don't have much confidence in your clan's investigative abilities to begin with. This place is a security nightmare. There's multiple access points on the compound an intruder could take advantage of. You're in the middle of a damn city making it near impossible to track everyone coming and going near the compound. As if that wasn't enough, part of your compound is open to the river. You don't have enough guards to patrol all the unsecure areas. Don't get me started on your antiquated surveillance technology."

Bethany took several swallows of water while she pondered his words. Security had never been an area she thought much about or paid attention to. Recent events made it clear changes should be made however. It didn't matter the city hadn't existed when her clan first built the compound here. The river had been selected because of their focus on shipbuilding. Something she *had* thought about. The world was changing, and her clan needed to adapt to the times. The shipping business wasn't as lucrative as it once was. Her clan would need to diversify and plan for the future. Whoever led the clan would need to be someone capable of accomplishing that. Apparently, they would need to address the security concerns as well.

Aaron was much more likely to want to keep the status quo than realize or listen to anyone advise him changes were needed. One more reason her cousin would not make a good ruler for the clan. Would Advisor Heyes make the better choice? He certainly appeared more reasonable and open to what was best for the clan. But could it all be a front to secure the vote?

"Should I be worried about your silence?"

Bethany glanced up at him.

"Experience has taught me women are more dangerous when they stop talking all together rather than screaming at me."

"Do women scream at you a lot?" It occurred to her she didn't really know much about his history.

Davis smirked. "Let's just say I've had my ears rung a time or two."

"Aunts? Sisters? Girlfriends?" He had mentioned he hadn't known his parents, but did he have other family members?

"Currently? No to all the above."

Bethany set her glass down in the sink and swiveled to face him. Should she ask him to elaborate? He didn't strike her as the sharing type, but loss had shaped her life. It continued to affect and manipulate her path. "I have no memory of either of my parents. They died when I was two. Bryant was nineteen years older than me. I realize for a Risharden that isn't much of a difference, but we were never close. I was sent to the Highlands to be raised by my nanny. Bryant stayed here, with Elsof, once he finished with his schooling in England."

Davis stared at the floor so long she thought he wouldn't speak. "Never knew my parents at all. My father died before I was born. My mother stayed around long enough to give birth to me but passed away shortly after to join her mate in the afterlife. At least that was what the old clan healer told me. The clan raised me.

Families pretty much took turns taking care of me."

Bethany laid a hand on his arm. "That must have been hard to understand as a child. You have no other family?"

He shrugged. "The clan is my family. It's all I've ever known. I had a much older sister, but she died before I was born, also. My parents were not young when they had me. The way I heard it, I was a bit of a surprise."

"I'm sure you were a very pleasant surprise. One of the downsides of our race is how rare children are. Each one is a precious blessing. There's nothing sweeter than a child's laughter, or purer than a baby's smile. Colin's visits always cheer my day."

Davis gazed down at the soft smile on her face. The yearning in her voice was evident. As her mate, only he could give her a child. Did she really have no idea her mate stood right next to her? The truth was so clear in his mind and heart. Did her innocence prevent her from seeing the truth? She knew Donald hadn't been her mate. Did she even suspect? Did he want her to?

Chapter Twelve

"I need to run." Davis ran his hands through his hair and paced the length of the room. "How do you manage in the city? It's not like you can fly around here. What do the members of your clan do?"

His movements became increasingly agitated. Living in the city certainly provided unique challenges to their race. Accustomed to the country, he probably had the freedom and luxury to shift as often as he liked. "Members of my clan change in the privacy of their homes if their altered form allows. There are also areas on the compound that accommodate those requiring more space. At the headquarters there are a group of ballrooms which are opened for clan members to use. They house a series of tunnels running beneath the compound as well for use. Some members own country homes to provide the outlet they need."

He stopped in mid-stride and jerked his head back. "Tunnels? There are tunnels running beneath this place? Are they patrolled? Do they enter and exit only on the compound?"

"I really don't know if they're patrolled. I never go down there. I do know there are exits outside of the compound."

Closing his eyes, he pinched the bridge of his nose and exhaled loudly. "I take it back, the security in this place isn't a nightmare, it's a complete joke." He swung around to face her and propped his fists on his hips. "Explains how Bryant managed to get out of here supposedly undetected."

Bethany clasped her hands behind her back and frowned slightly. "I imagine you are correct. It does appear our security is sadly lacking. However, you shouldn't form your opinions based on my knowledge of the security measures of the clan. There may be patrols, but I simply am not informed on the matter."

"I'm not. I arrived at the conclusion by witnessing most of it firsthand. The tunnels' existence are just the nails in the coffin."

"Aaron oversees the security. I doubt very much he would speak to you on the subject, however, or listen to your opinions."

Davis rolled his eyes. "Of course, he is. The news just keeps getting better. Why didn't I know that? I'll have to check with Malcolm, but I don't recall that being mentioned before either."

"It's not an official title. I believe Uncle Elsof was giving him a trial period at the position. A chance to learn the procedures and demonstrate his ability to rule."

He snorted. "Yeah, I think the answer to that is an emphatic no."

"You believe Advisor Heyes would make a better ruler?"

"I believe a monkey would probably make a better ruler than your cousin, but that doesn't mean I'm a fan of Heyes either. The jury is still out on that one as far as I'm concerned."

Bethany tried not to smile, but her lips twitched in response. Unfortunately, she had to acknowledge Aaron would not make an effective leader.

"You never shared what you do when you have the need to fly?"

"Oh, I go to the Highlands, where I spent my childhood. I still own the family home there. I inherited it from my parents. Bryant was already an adult when they died and had no interest in the Highland property. He preferred the city. You know, it's rather similar to your home in Wyoming. The mountains aren't quite as tall, but it is breathtakingly beautiful. Plenty of room for you to run."

"Is that an invitation?"

She opened her mouth to refuse. They couldn't possibly go. Turmoil embroiled her clan. Someone was using her brother's scent blocker.

Pressing her lips together, she stared down at the tiny bows on the tips of her ballet slippers. What difference would her presence make? If the vote happened, and it looked like it would, then it wouldn't take place in the next day or two. A few days away would give her time to think without the pressure of Aaron or Advisor Heyes courting her to their side. As for the one who attacked her? Maybe during her time away, they would catch them. It would at least provide a little breathing room between Davis and her. As long as he insisted on assigning himself to be her bodyguard, the more space they had the better. Her cottage wasn't overly large, but it was certainly a great deal bigger than her flat.

She glanced up to find Davis patiently waiting for her response. "I suppose it is. A day or two at the cottage sounds a bit heavenly right now."

****

"As we crest the hill, you will be able to see the loch."

Davis glanced in Bethany's direction. She was angled away from him staring out the passenger window. The last one hundred kilometers of the trip had passed with little conversation—only a brief sentence or two about a village they passed through. As the elevation had risen, so had the silence.

His thoughts swirled around the danger surrounding her like a rattlesnake coiled and ready to strike. Murder and violence had set up shop on her doorstep, and he was damned if they would get inside and do her harm. She was his mate. Even though he wasn't ready to claim her, he wasn't about to leave her unprotected. The more remote the scenery grew outside the window, the less urgent the danger seemed. Maybe it would give him a chance to work through the layers and figure out who had been working with her brother. He knew one thing—he had to keep from touching her again.

The deep blue depths of the loch appeared over the horizon. Verdant grass edged the shore and climbed the base of the gray craggy hills. His foot eased off the gas.

"Now this is more my kind of scene."

Davis pulled off to the side to take in the view.

"I imagine this more closely resembles your clan's compound in Wyoming. I confess my perception was impaired during my stay, therefore I did not stop to admire the beauty of my surroundings."

"You'll have to go back. There are some places so remote in the mountains that few humans ever see. Panoramic vistas both humbling and awe inspiring."

"You really love it there, don't you?"

He glanced at her before turning his gaze back to the road and continuing on their way. "It's a part of me."

"I feel that way about my clan, too. I used to believe it was the Risharden way, but I realize now not everyone feels the same way."

"I think it's part of our nature as Rishardens to stay close to our clans, but just like humans there will be the outliers. Some feel the urge to roam. Some move off the compound but are still relatively nearby. Others can't get away fast or far enough."

"Yes, I suppose you are right. There are those on the opposite spectrum as well in my clan. A few members have never even left the city compound."

"Yeah, we too have those.

"Take the next left. It's a narrow, unpaved road with limited travelers, but if we do encounter a vehicle you will have to pull over to let them pass." Bethany leaned forward and pointed. "There it is."

Davis took the turn. "How much farther?"

"About three kilometers down will be my driveway on the left. It's a bit rough. Small stone pillars and a stone wall mark the entrance."

Spirals of rock jutted up from the ground like fingers pointing to the sky. The mountains here resembled ancient Gods, a bit worn down from the millennia but powerful all the same.

"There's the turn up ahead. Just past the cluster of purple heather. In a month or so the hills will be covered with flowers. It's quite a stunning sight."

The deeply rutted dirt path made it impossible to travel above a crawl. The farther they travelled down it the closer Bethany leaned in her seat to the window.

Davis smiled over her eagerness.

A small, white cottage appeared in view. Two narrow dormers with a single window in each jutted from the roof of the second story. A stone wall flanked its sides, the hills and mountains dwarfed the building behind its back, and the loch edged the front. An old, crumbling stone building resided in the distance. Trees surrounded the cottage encapsulating it in privacy. Clumps of yellow flowers fanned the yard. He pulled to a stop, and Bethany jumped out before he put the car in park.

She took a deep breath, and a wide grin lit up her face. The sun bathed her upturned face in light, making her light blonde hair incandescent.

Opening the car door, the eerily familiar mountain air filled his senses. It had the same chilly bite, unpolluted purity, and earthy undertones as home. The dark blue water was vast, and he imagined deep and as frigid as ice.

Bethany entered the cottage through a forest green door. Getting out of the car, Davis stood and stretched his arms over his head and cracked his back before following her inside. A narrow staircase led upstairs. A living area was to his left. Bethany's soft tread was coming from the back of the building, so he followed the narrow hallway to what opened to a kitchen and dining area stretching across the back. A small, round, pine table and chairs with a glass vase in the center holding dried heather occupied the left side. On the right, an ancient looking white fridge and oven took up the entire side wall, and a white farm sink and cabinets spanned the back wall. Glass doors by the table opened onto a stone patio so any occupants could enjoy the splendor of the loch.

"Are you hungry? I can't offer you anything fresh, but I keep the freezer and cabinets well stocked." She stood in front of the open cabinet with a soft smile.

"I'm good. What I'd really like to do is run. Is there anything I need to worry about? Any area I should avoid?"

"Oh, no, this side of the loch is uninhabited except for us. The Highlands are one of the most scarcely populated areas in Europe. Although there is always the danger of a trespasser, it's highly unlikely, and I have never encountered one."

"Great." He started to march out the patio doors, but hesitated. "You'll be okay here?"

"Of course. Take as long as you need. I am perfectly safe here. I can hear anyone approaching from quite the distance. The loch amplifies the sound, I believe, and my own hearing is rather pronounced."

Davis nodded and walked out onto the patio.

Bethany turned back to the white wooden cabinets and closed them. Her appetite was nonexistent as well. She'd worry about food later. Traipsing through the archway into the living area, she trailed her hand over the dusty, rustic furniture. She had sat in this rocking chair losing herself in book after book as a child, letting the stories carry her away to far off lands and meet eccentric characters. She couldn't help but smile. So many memories filled these rooms. Loneliness and a desire to connect with her family and clan members had prompted her to move to the compound. Duty to the clan, her job, and newfound friends convinced her to remain there.

Upstairs, she checked two bedrooms and promptly

decided the single downstairs bedroom would suit Davis better. The roofline, although fine for her, was too low up here for him to be comfortable with his height. Besides, the only privy in the home was downstairs next to the bedroom. It would also give them both a little privacy and breathing room after sharing their previous tight confines.

The bedroom with the small window with a view of the loch had been hers as a child. The small, gray, wooden desk beneath the window had been where she sat to do her lessons. Bethany peeked out the window at the rowan tree growing in the yard. The graceful tree stood tall and narrow. In a few months, its leaves would turn red and the berries would ripen. She remembered her nanny harvesting the berries to make jelly.

Wandering back downstairs, she walked into the bedroom. She doubted the floral wallpaper and area rug, or the pink sheets and white bedspread edged with lace were his style, but it was still the largest room. Peeking into the privy, she checked to make certain the ivory pedestal sink and clawfoot tub were functioning properly. After a slight hesitation, the water gushed out. Baths were probably not his thing either, but there was a shower attachment. She fluffed the light pink towels on the rack and smiled slightly. The image of Davis using the feminine privy both amused and enticed her.

Fetching a duster from the cabinet under the sink in the kitchen, she got rid of the dust coating the ground floor. A caretaker came to check on the property periodically. Bethany wasn't able to spend as much time here as she would like because of her job. But during the summer months, she usually took a few long weekends to holiday here. Satisfied Davis would be comfortable enough, she stepped out onto the patio.

He had been in quite a hurry. His clothes were dropped haphazardly across the stones. Bethany chuckled as she stooped to gather and fold his clothes before placing them neatly on the stone bench facing the loch.

Plucking a few weeds which had managed to grow between the flat stones, she mused over the times she had played with her toys on the patio as a child.

She sat down on the bench and tilted her face up to feel the crisp air. It was so pure here. No smell of exhaust or factory pollution tainted the air. Only the sounds of water gently lapping at the rocky shore and the faint rustle of leaves as a soft breeze blew intruded on the quiet. A piece of dark driftwood bobbed in the water. A brown buzzard flew overhead, searching for prey no doubt.

The sudden urge to fly gripped her. Bethany stood and started removing her clothing. She folded her clothes neatly and stacked them next to Davis' on the bench. She raised her face to the sky and stretched her arms wide. Energy rippled over her body as she willed herself to transform. The change took only seconds.

A small leap to the bench, and a flap of her wings made her airborne. She flew straight up over the cottage and circled around—peering down at the old stone ruins behind her cottage. It was the site of the original dwelling on this property, old and crumbling long before her time. The only parts remaining were remnants of the chimney and portions of two of the outer gray stone walls. Vegetation and wildlife had claimed it for their own. She flew higher, heading up farther into the hills. As a child she had fashioned many a fort in the hills. Being the only child in the area, she had learned to entertain herself.

Her nanny hadn't been a cruel woman, but neither was she a warm and cuddly one either. Distant was the most appropriate word. She had done her duty to raise Bethany and had left once the duty was completed. She had been one of the unblessed, a Risharden unable to shift. It happened to a few every generation. Bethany liked to believe the stigma attached to the unblessed had lessened over the years, but they often were ostracized and viewed as flawed. Nanny never spoke about it, so she didn't know if it had bothered her one way or the other. Bethany had only found out Nanny was one of the unblessed after overhearing a conversation between her uncle and brother after she herself had made the transformation for the first time—alone.

Risharden first shifted after they hit puberty. Being on her own most of the time, she had been hesitant and a bit afraid of making the switch for the first time. The trick was not to fight the change. It could become uncomfortable and even painful if you didn't relax into the shift. She had been sixteen before shifting the first time, a little late compared to most Risharden. Her delayed transformation had been the topic of the overheard conversation. Her brother had made a nasty joke about him fearing being unblessed could be contagious and the reason why she hadn't yet changed. As if her nanny being one of the unblessed had made her one of them.

As the sun began its descent toward the horizon, Bethany flew back home and landed on a branch next to the house overlooking the patio. Davis' clothes remained on the bench. He must be still out on his run. She rotated her head to watch the sunset over the mountains in the distance.

The bright orange ball of fire bordered by ribbons of pink and lilac put on a spectacular show. The soft thump of padded feet and pants drew her attention back to the patio. A large grayish-brown wolf trotted up onto the patio. He stopped in the center and glanced toward the cottage and then back toward the loch. She supposed it was a very good thing they were in a remote location. Wolves hadn't been seen around here for centuries. Just when she believed he hadn't noticed her perching in the tree, he angled his head up and pinned her with his yellow tinged gaze.

He shook, and his fur morphed into skin. His long, sinewy form rested on all fours before he stood straight and tall. She should probably look away and give him his privacy, but her gaze was trapped by his powerful body. She was riveted to his every movement as he raised an arm to brush back the hair from his eyes.

Unabashed by his nakedness, he stood with his hands on his hips gazing into her eyes. Most Risharden were accustomed to being naked in front of others but having grown up in relative solitude Bethany was generally much more circumspect about changing.

Davis' gaze remained locked on her. He was waiting.

Feeling somehow more exposed as an owl under his watchful gaze, she glided down to the patio, changing smoothly as she landed in front of the bench. She immediately bent to grab her clothes only for Davis to take her hand.

She swallowed audibly and met his gaze.

Releasing her hand, he raised both of his hands to cradle her face. The sun dipped below the horizon as his head lowered and took her lips in a tender kiss.

His soft lips molded to hers as he deepened the kiss and stepped closer to her, brushing his body against hers. Warmth spread over her, and she raised her hands to touch him. The soft hair on his chest tickled her palms as she smoothed them over his muscles.

The spicy taste of him bloomed in her mouth as his tongue made gentle forays to tangle with hers. His hands began a slow exploration of her body.

Bethany gasped when he cupped her breasts and rubbed his thumbs over her erect nipples.

His mouth continued to devour hers. Rivers of sensation coursed through her body. She strained closer to him.

Suddenly, the world tilted as he swung her up into his arms and strode into the cottage. She looped her arms around his shoulders and hung on as he managed to open the door without dropping her.

"Which way?" He paused inside the kitchen and gazed down at her.

Words wouldn't come so she pointed toward the bedroom door. He angled sideways to fit them through the door and stalked over to the double bed. He lowered her to her feet briefly while he pulled back the white quilted bedspread and pink sheet. Grasping her by the waist, he easily lifted her.

She gasped at the movement and the cool sheets against her skin as he laid her down. She scooted back, feeling shy and unsure of herself. Before doubts could creep in and take hold, Davis was there leaning over her, capturing her lips once again.

Clutching his shoulders, Bethany reveled in his kiss.

Davis trailed a line of kisses down her neck and chest. The soft abrasion of his five o'clock shadow tingled against her sensitized breasts. She arched against him when he took her into his hot mouth. He paid them both devout attention.

She squirmed against him in need. Soft pants escaped her as she kneaded his shoulders and arms.

A thick thigh slid between her legs and opened her to him. His hand made a slow, lazy advance down her abdomen.

Turning her head, she bit her lip as his long fingers flitted over her and alternated between a delicate strumming motion and pressing deep inside her. Her eyes drifted closed as her nerves became awash in pleasure.

She needed more. She needed him.

Bethany's hands smoothed down his torso. He stiffened and let out a harsh groan when her fingers wrapped around him. Before she could explore his length, he nudged her hand away, slid between her thighs, and entered her slowly.

His gaze blazed into hers until they were fully joined. She pulled his head down to kiss him thoroughly while they both moved as one.

The orgasm washed over her like a tidal wave, leaving her gasping and arching against him. He clutched her to him as it propelled him toward his own fulfillment.

Their breaths intermingled as they each rode the waves of pleasure to completion.

As Davis rolled to his side and wrapped an arm

around her shoulders to pull her to his chest, Bethany glanced down and started to giggle.

"Well that's not a comforting reaction." His voice rumbled over her head, and her eyes shot wide as she realized what he meant.

She peeked up at him, unabashedly laughing. "I really don't think low confidence is an issue for you, but just in case, it was the sight of your toes dangling off the bed which set me to laughing not...anything else."

Davis lifted his head to glance down at the end of the bed. "I suppose this is the longest bed in the place?"

"I am afraid so. I thought this room would be the most comfortable since the upstairs has low ceilings and well, you are tall."

"I guess you'll just have to distract me from your short bed." He lifted her chin and kissed her, sending any response she might have given him right out of her head.

Chapter Thirteen

The enticing scent of baking bread roused him from sleep. Davis stretched and listened to the soft humming coming from the kitchen. He dropped his head back to the pillow and closed his eyes.

He hadn't meant to touch her, at least that was the lie he told himself. As soon as he'd seen her shift from the light brown owl with the white heart shaped face into the slim little angel with the halo of pale blonde hair, he knew he was lost. He had to touch her soft skin. Kiss those pouty lips.

Groaning, he rubbed a hand over his face. That train of thought would lead him straight into the kitchen to drag her back to bed.

He swung his legs over the side and sat up, hanging his head and twisting it side to side until he heard the telltale crack. He couldn't take it back, not that he would, so there was no point in belaboring over a deed already done. What he needed to focus on was where did they go from here? He'd crossed the line he set for himself. Touching her would only make it harder to walk away. His loyalty was to his clan. They were the one constant in his life, his family. He couldn't walk away from them. Not even for a mate.

Compounding the problem, he hadn't worn a condom. Normally it wasn't an issue. Risharden didn't get or carry any of the diseases humans did, and pregnancy wasn't typically a worry either. Unless you had sex with your mate that is. Damn it, what if she was pregnant?

Bethany couldn't possibly expect to raise their child in the midst of her crazy clan, could she? No way was he letting that happen. She would have to move to his clan. Hell, she'd be as miserable away from her clan as he would be away from his.

The chances of her being pregnant were slim. They weren't exactly a fertile race. One night shouldn't cause her to conceive. All the more reason he needed to keep his hands off of her.

Davis stood and looked around for his clothes. Right, he'd left them outside last night and he'd never taken his duffle bag out of the car. He sighed and walked the length of the bed, almost tripping over his duffle on the floor at the foot of the bed. Grimacing slightly, he bent over to lift it to the bed. Bethany must have carried it in.

After ruffling through his bag for some clean clothes, he moved to the only other door in the room besides the one which opened into the kitchen. He really hoped it was to the bathroom and not a closet.

Bethany opened the oven door to check the bread. The top had baked a warm honey brown color. She smiled and donned an oven mitt to remove it from the oven to cool. There was something about the warm scent of fresh baked bread she found soothing. Perhaps the smell evoked pleasant memories of her childhood. Her nanny had often had some tantalizing treat baking in the oven or cooling on the counter.

The sound of the water turning on caused her to glance toward the bedroom. She'd heard him moving about a brief time ago and wondered if or when he would make an appearance and how they would act with one another now. Would he kiss her good morning?

Had last night changed anything? It had for her. It had been everything she had always envisioned making love to be. The giddy feeling of joy bubbling inside her. The breathless wonder of passion sweeping over her. The satiated calm and comfort of the aftermath as he held her in his arms before sleep claimed them both.

She rested her hands on the counter and stared out the window at the loch. Did it mean Davis was her mate? Had she found her other half? Could it be the reason why she had always been drawn to him? Why he made her feel safe? Did he know?

The bedroom door opened behind her, and she whirled around with a ready smile. He stepped over the threshold and then stared out the window at the loch. His damp hair clung to his neck. A black T-shirt stretched across his shoulders.

"Good morning."

He mumbled, "morning" back at her without glancing in her direction.

Maybe he wasn't a morning person. Perhaps coffee might help. "Would you like some coffee? I'm afraid it's instant. Is that all right?"

He gave an absent wave of his hand in her direction. "I'll make some in a while. I'm going to head outside for a bit."

Davis sauntered outside and down to the shore. She stood at the window staring at him. He faced the loch with his hands in the front pockets of his blue jeans. Something was wrong. He regretted last night. That had to be it. What else could it be?

Bethany wiped down the counter and sink and then moseyed into the bedroom and privy to tidy up in there. If he suspected she was his mate, as she did, then he wasn't happy about the development. He didn't want her for a mate. She looked up from wiping the pedestal sink into the wooden oval mirror above. Her pale reflection stared back at her.

Well, who could blame him? It wasn't exactly an ideal match for him, now was it? She was the sister of the man who had murdered Davis' friend and tried to murder the mate of the leader of his clan. It must seem like a cruel trick of fate for him to be saddled with a mate who was surrounded by violence and death.r

Bethany shuffled into the bedroom and plopped down on the edge of the bed. A tear dropped down onto her hand. A shuddered breath escaped her before she tightly closed her eyes and clenched her hands together in her lap. Once again, she was a fool.

Rejection, a common theme in her life. Like a defective tool, used and cast away. Her family saw her as either useless or a pawn. Growing up in relative isolation, she had been somewhat socially awkward when thrust into the social quagmire of university. It had taken some time to adjust and eventually learn to navigate with any success. Her first crush had been a boy who worked in the library where she went to study. He had been shy like her. He had this adorable habit of pushing his spectacles up his nose with the pad of his thumb. She had spent many an hour musing over him instead of her studies. After finally gathering up the nerve to speak to him, she had discovered they shared a common major in engineering. Being two years ahead of her, she thought asking him to tutor her would provide the perfect opportunity to grow closer. And it had, at first—in the end he had made it clear she was simply a paycheck to him. He had no interest in any other relationship. The sting of that rejection still smarted. She had eschewed trying to date after that, until Donald.

Wiping her cheeks, she crossed into the privy and splashed some cool water on her face. Enough. Wallowing in misery never produced anything but more misery. She would not make this more difficult for either of them. She would follow his lead and keep a distance between them. There was no reason they couldn't be civil to one another. She had hoped to spend another day here, but perhaps it would be better if they returned to the city today. He had to see the assault had been an isolated incident. She had simply been in the wrong place at the wrong time. He could continue with his clan business, and she could get back to work and her life.

Bethany gripped the privy door handle for a moment and breathed deeply. Walking slowly through the bedroom, she made her way into the kitchen. All the time, listening for any sound of his possible arrival. She wanted to be composed and not caught unaware when he returned. She glanced out the window but he was no longer there. Only the gentle waves of the water met her view. He probably wanted to take advantage of another run. Her shoulders dropped, and she gave a small sigh. Good. It gave her a short reprieve. Some time to prepare herself to paste a smile on her face and pretend her heart didn't hurt.

Chapter Fourteen

"Thank you, Lady Bethany, you always know what to do."

Bethany smiled warmly at her neighbor, Bridget. "That is unfortunately not accurate, but I am happy I could help in this situation." She took a sip of her tea from the delicate china tea cup and glanced at the bright green parakeet in its golden cage in the corner of the room. The older woman had knocked on her door early this morning in a panic after finding an empty cage. She tended to forget to latch the door properly and would periodically come begging for help in locating her precious pet, Oscar. Luckily, Bethany's hearing proved to be an immense help pinpointing the bird's location. This time the parakeet had been nesting in the closet on the top shelf. One time, it had managed to escape the flat, and she had to chase it all over the building before cornering it in the top stairwell.

"I need to be getting to work. Is there anything I can do for you before I go?" She stood and carried her cup to the kitchen.

"After all the excitement I think I'm going to sit here and rest until my stories come on."

"Then I'm off. Have a wonderful day."

Waving goodbye, Bethany left her neighbor's flat and walked down the hall to her own. She still had some time before work, but she might as well go in a few minutes early. After a quick stop to grab her purse, she relocked the flat.

The sun was already bright and warming up the day when she stepped out of her building. She glanced up to see not a cloud in the blue sky. Any rain in the forecast would be holding off at least for the morning.

She hadn't seen Davis for two days. They had returned from the Highlands and either he had agreed she wasn't in any danger or he had taken the excuse to distance himself from her, but either way he no longer considered himself her bodyguard. She knew he hadn't left the compound because her friends Celeste and Kate had visited her yesterday and filled her in on all the places he'd been spotted and the gossip running rampant throughout the clan about his purpose for still being there. It ran the gamut from him being a spy and part of a clan takeover, to him defecting to their clan. Bethany had simply stated he was here on council business because of the turmoil in the clan. She had continued to say, once a new leader was determined, she was sure he would return to his own clan.

Bethany saw no point in worrying her friends over the possibility of Bryant having had an accomplice who might or might not be still active. It was still just a theory Davis had. There had been no more incidents she knew of. Certainly, none involving her.

She nodded and smiled at the clan members who greeted her as she strolled down the pavement to the office building. A vote had been scheduled in two weeks to decide the fate of the clan and its leadership—despite Aaron's claims the right to rule was his and his alone. It looked like he would have no choice but to go along with the clan's decision. He didn't have enough of the guards backing him to enforce his claims. She couldn't help but be a bit worried over his reaction if he didn't win the vote.

Entering the building, she smiled as she approached the security desk. "Good morning, Walter. How is Colleen and the precious bundle she is carrying?"

"I believe she is in full-on nesting mode, Lady Bethany. She's been a little whirlwind decorating the nursery."

She signed her name in the security log. "That is wonderful. Tell her I said hello, would you?"

"I will, and welcome back. It's a pleasure to see you return to work with us."

"Thank you."

Bethany crossed the lobby to the elevators and rode to the design floor. Her return was greeted with more fanfare than she had anticipated. In truth, she hadn't expected more than the occasional *welcome back* but she hadn't anticipated everyone's insatiable curiosity about Bryant, Davis, or her knowledge and role with both. One after one, they'd approached or stopped her as she haltingly traversed the maze of gray cubicles to hers tucked away in the corner. A few circled her small cubicle peppering her with questions as she put away her things in the bottom drawer of her desk and scanned the workspace for anything which may have been added or removed during her absence. She absently answered them with inane murmurs and evasions.

Kate arrived to shoo them all away and commandeer Bethany's attention. She sat on the corner of Bethany's heavy metal desk with her arms folded and peered down at her.

"Didn't expect the curiosity horde, did you?"

Bethany shook her head and gave her a wan smile.

"Tell them to mind their own business." She waved an elegant hand with red-tipped nails in their direction. "Now, that's them. For me, I still want all the juicy details." She leaned in close and gave Bethany a wide-eyed expectant stare.

"I already told you and Celeste about Bryant and Davis."

"Did you? I get the feeling there's more than what you told us. Are you holding out on us?"

"Holding out on who?" Celeste appeared in Bethany's cubicle wearing a short lilac skirt and peach silk blouse, holding a tray of beverages. She placed them down on the desk and handed one to Bethany. "Here's your tea, and Kate your coffee is the one on the right."

"I'm cutting back on my coffee intake. Since I've already had two cups this morning I better not."

"Oh, poo, I didn't know." Celeste pouted.

"I made the decision this morning." Kate waved her hand in the air dismissively.

"Would you like my tea? I had my fill this morning. I helped Bridget with her bird, and she gave me a cup after I had already had one at home."

"Sure, why not, I'll give it a try and see if I can convert." Kate lifted the cup and wrinkled her nose after taking a sip. "Really doesn't compare. There's no kick to the system." She shrugged. "Well at least there's some caffeine in it. Wean me off the coffee." She glanced at Celeste. "There is caffeine in this, right? Never mind, don't tell me. I prefer to blindly believe there is."

Bethany chuckled, and Celeste just stood there staring at Kate as she gulped the tea.

"I suppose I better get to work. I'll see you two for lunch, and Bethany be forewarned I will expect more details about your little jaunt to the country with that sexy American." Kate raised her cup in salute as she sauntered away.

Celeste watched her for a moment before turning back to Bethany. "What's she talking about?"

Bethany forced a smile and a shrug. She hadn't told them about sleeping with Davis or believing him to be her mate. She wasn't ready to share that information yet. They were her best friends, but just thinking about discussing it made her cringe. She knew they would be supportive, but they both had men trailing after them. How could they commiserate on being rejected—not just by anyone, but your mate? The one who was supposed to love you above all others. The one who was meant to desire and cherish you. Not the one who awakened you and calmly walked away as if it meant nothing.

"I better get going, too. Tootles, see you at lunch."

Her friend sashayed away. Bethany swiveled her chair back to her desk. Burying herself in work was just the distraction she needed. At first, the multiple conversations, tapping on the keyboards, opening and closing of metal drawers overwhelmed her senses, but soon she relaxed into the familiarity of the noise and tuned it out.

A few hours later, a murmuring drew her attention from the computer. She peeked over the top edge of her cubicle to see a cluster of people by the windows staring down. The rough texture of the cubicle wall scraped against her palms as she strained higher to see. Something was happening. She sighed and briefly thought about slumping back into her chair and ignoring the commotion. If it concerned her, eventually she would find out. Did she really want to involve herself in more drama right now?

Before she could decide, Maureen, one of her co-workers sidled up to her. "You're friends with that Kate in legal, aren't you?"

Bethany refrained from stating the obvious. Maureen knew she was. "Why?"

"She got sick. They're carrying her out now."

Bethany surged to her feet. "What! What happened?"

She ran to the window with Maureen trailing behind her. "As I said, she's sick. They called the healer in, and they're transporting now."

Pushing her way to the window, she looked down to see one of the guards carry Kate out of the building and approach a waiting guard's vehicle. She looked unconscious. Watching intently to detect any movement from her friend, her heart clenched in her chest. The guard bent and placed her in the backseat. Kate hadn't moved.

Bethany whirled away and ran to her desk to grab her purse and pull out her cell phone. She hesitated briefly between the stairs and elevator. The elevators would take too much time. She dialed Celeste as she jogged down the stairs. The staccato of her heels tapping the concrete steps echoed up the stairwell.

Celeste picked up on the first ring. "Oh my gosh, Bethany, there's something wrong with Kate!"

"I just heard. I saw them put her in the car. What

do you know?"

"She started vomiting and collapsed is all I heard. The healer arrived and is taking her to medical."

"No idea why?"

"No."

Bethany entered the lobby and jogged across as fast as heels would allow. "I'm leaving the building now. Where are you?"

"Oh, of course, I'm coming too." Celeste disconnected the phone.

Bouncing to a stop, Bethany balanced on one leg to remove one shoe and then the other. She stuffed them into her purse as best as she could. The heels hung over the side. She clutched her purse under her arm and sprinted out the door and down the road. The rough cobblestones scraped against her bare feet, and were hot from the sun, but her only thought was to reach her friend.

Medical resided in one of the smaller buildings by the entrance. Risharden didn't often get sick, so it wasn't much more than a couple of rooms on the ground floor. The healer's flat took up the remainder of the floor.

Bethany ran across the square to the brick building. People turned to stare, but she didn't care or stop. The guards she had seen taking Kate from the office building were exiting as she ran up. They held the door. She didn't pause to question them what they knew. The door opened into the empty waiting room.

Opening the door to the examining room, she searched the room. Elizabeth, the healer, looked up and exclaimed, "Lady Bethany!"

"How is she?" Bethany stared at her friend lying

unconscious on the exam table. Her skin was stark white. She released her tight grip on the door handle and approached the table.

Elizabeth frowned and returned her attention to Kate. "She's been poisoned."

Gasping, Bethany grasped the edge of the table. "Poisoned?"

"Yes, she's ingested fallibar. How or why, I do not know. My concern is how much?"

"Fallibar? Is it…deadly?"

Elizabeth briefly glanced up. "It's a plant native to our home world. We transported samples with us because it is used for medicinal purposes in tiny doses. See these purple striations around her mouth? That tells me it's fallibar."

Elizabeth's competent hands continued to examine Kate. Only the small upward and downward movements of her friend's chest telling her she still lived kept Bethany's panic at bay. Who could have done this, and why? Who could possibly want to hurt Kate? Had her friend come across something at work? She was a lawyer and privy to secrets.

The heavy outer door squeaked as it was opened, and Celeste called her name. "In here, Celeste."

Celeste hesitantly opened the door and peeked inside. When she spotted Kate on the table, she burst into noisy tears. Bethany walked over and hugged her.

"Take her outside."

Bethany frowned, but followed Elizabeth's instructions and steered Celeste out of the room with an arm around her shaking shoulders. She didn't want to impede Elizabeth's examination by arguing or disturbing her with Celeste's sobbing. Comforting her friend by giving her a shoulder to cry on and rubbing her back, she kept glancing at the exam room door trying to listen for any clue to Kate's fate.

The pale green walls displayed landscape paintings. The brown-cloth chairs were comfortable enough. An assortment of plants, from tall green leaves to bright red flowers, were strewn about the room. All were probably meant to comfort and soothe, but she had to fight the urge to spring to her feet and demand entrance to the exam room.

Although it seemed like hours, the constant glances at the clock told her it had been less than one when Elizabeth stepped out of the exam room. Celeste had calmed down to hiccupping sniffles and clutched Bethany's hand with her own.

"I've given her medicine to counteract the poison. I won't know for sure until she wakes, but I believe she will make a full recovery."

Bethany fell back against the chair and closed her eyes. *Thank you. Thank you. Thank you.*

She opened her eyes and leaned forward, staring intently into Elizabeth's earnest gaze. "Can we see her?"

Glancing back and forth between Celeste and Bethany, Elizabeth pursed her dark red lips. The smooth, caramel skin of her forehead wrinkled in thought. She gave a sharp nod. "As long as you don't disturb her. She needs rest now."

Bethany nodded and stood, pulling Celeste up with her. "Is she awake?"

"Not yet, but her pulse and breathing are much stronger. I need to notify the guards outside."

Celeste gasped. "The guards? What for?"

"I doubt she put the poison in her tea herself. Someone poisoned her. The guards need to investigate."

Celeste fell back into her chair, knocking Bethany off balance. She stumbled and flailed an arm out to steady herself with a palm against the wall.

"Tea?" she whispered.

"Yes, I took the cup off her desk and tested the contents. The fallibar was in the tea, along with some other ingredients I haven't identified yet. Until I do, I cannot be certain about her recovery."

Elizabeth walked away. Celeste hyperventilated behind her, but she couldn't turn her body to offer her solace. She was frozen in place.

The poison was in the tea Celeste had brought. The tea meant for her.

Chapter Fifteen

Bethany cradled Kate's hand in hers as she stood next to the cushioned, beige examination table. Celeste sat on an orange plastic chair in the corner of the room shredding a tissue in her lap. The monotony of the white walls was broken only by a single painting of a starry night sky, and the window on the opposite side looking out onto a small courtyard. Two small rows of herbal gardens were in the center. Heavy brown curtains hung at the window. Squeezing her eyes tightly closed to stem the tears threatening to fall, she blinked them open and gazed down at her friend.

Kate still hadn't awoken yet.

A commotion erupted outside the exam room. Two guards had been placed to guard Kate. Bethany stared at the door. Her hand involuntarily tightened on Kate's. Was whoever put the poison in the tea trying to finish the job?

"Get the fuck out of my way!"

She sagged into herself. Davis was here.

The sound of a body slamming into the wall had her take a step forward to intervene. Before she could, the door swung open to reveal Davis standing in the opening—his gaze cataloging the room before it settled on her, raking her from head to foot.

Bethany glanced at the guards scrambling up from the floor where he had apparently plowed through them. Her lips trembled when her gaze collided with his. She pressed them together and raised her chin.

Davis' heart pounded so hard it felt like it would leap from his chest. When he heard someone had been poisoned at the office building, his breath had seized in his lungs. Even after learning it had been Kate, not Bethany, he had to confirm it for himself. He had to see her with his own eyes and know she was okay. He knew she would be by her friend's side.

Her skin was pale, her eyes glistened, and he caught the slight trembling before she straightened her spine. His heart told him to take her in his arms to comfort the both of them, but his head argued that it was a slippery slope he needed to stay the hell off of.

She glanced away, and his head won the argument.

The guards gained their feet and surged into the room. He pivoted to meet their attack. Landing a few punches was just what he needed to get rid of the frustration eating at his gut.

Bethany stepped forward to intervene, waving a hand at the guards. The fact they both immediately stepped down both impressed and irritated him at the same time.

"Mr. Campbell is with me. Please excuse his abrupt methods. In the future, please allow him immediate access to wherever I am."

The guards both nodded before casting a glare toward him and spinning on their heels to leave— closing the door behind them.

She hurried back to Kate's side, smoothing the blanket covering her, and giving her hand a slight squeeze. He glanced at Celeste sitting in the corner sniffling and staring at a shredded tissue in her lap and back to Bethany.

"What happened?"

She rubbed her forehead and closed her eyes. "The healer said someone put fallibar in the tea she drank. It's a plant from—"

"I know what it is. Do they know who did it? Will she recover?"

Before she could answer, a woman stepped into the room from another doorway. Her long cornrows hairstyle swung with her movements. Sedate navy pants were topped by a fire engine red top. Her chocolate gaze swept the room before she examined Kate.

"You are the American visitor I presume?" She glanced up at him while she shone a light into Kate's eyes.

He nodded.

"This is Davis Campbell. Davis, this Elizabeth Deveraux, our clan healer." Bethany introduced them as if they were at some formal engagement. He wanted answers not introductions.

"What's her prognosis?"

The healer stared at him, clearly debating whether to tell him anything. She clasped her hands in front of her body and twiddled her thumbs.

"Davis is here on council business. You can speak freely in front of him."

"Very well. I'm currently running tests on blood, saliva, and skin samples. They will take some time. I'm also doing a more thorough analysis of the tea she ingested. While I am confident fallibar was used, I need to ensure I have all the data available to make an accurate diagnosis. Her vitals have improved, but as you can see, she is still unconscious. I have treated her for the fallibar poisoning, but if she was given something else in addition, I cannot treat it without first identifying the ingredient."

Folding his arms across his chest, Davis stared at the top of Bethany's head as she anxiously watched her friend. It would be quite a coincidence if her attack and Kate's poisoning weren't somehow related, but not entirely impossible. But why poison Kate?

"Umm, Elizabeth, I was recently poisoned. I am not sure if it could be the same poison or have any similarities. It made me terribly ill and weak. I do not know what was used. Would speaking to the North American clan's healer help at all?"

The healer stopped her examination and stared at Bethany. "Was fallibar used?"

"I don't know." Bethany glanced at Davis. "Do you recall any purple marks around my mouth when I was found?"

He shook his head. She obviously thought the poisonings were related somehow, or maybe she was trying to grasp at straws in an effort to help her friend. Did she have more information?

The healer pinned her dark gaze on him. "She was found unconscious? How long? Symptoms? Anna Blake is your healer is she not?"

"Anna died a few years ago. Ashley Parnassus is our healer now. I can call her if you want to speak to her." He looked at Bethany. "Why do you think it could be the same?"

Bethany twisted her fingers together. "I believe it is best to pursue any possibility if it might help Kate, don't you?"

"Call her."

Davis glanced at the healer after she voiced her demand and pulled the phone from his pocket. Bethany was holding something back. He dialed Ashley's number while staring at Bethany. Maybe she didn't want to speak in front of an audience, but he would get to the bottom of this.

"Well, well, how's Scotland, wolf boy?" He grinned. It was good to hear a voice from home, even if she was using the dreaded nickname she dubbed him with as a child.

"Hey, Ash, I'm with the clan healer here, and she has some questions about the poison used on Bethany. Do you know—"

The healer grabbed his phone and started talking. "What were her symptoms? Did you analyze samples?" She marched over to a counter which stretched along the wall and pulled some paper and a pen from a drawer and started writing things down.

He stepped closer to Bethany. "What aren't you telling me?"

She peeked up at him and then away. "The tea was intended for me. I didn't want it, so I offered it to Kate and she drank it."

Son of a bitch!

Clenching his fists, he wanted to swing around and punch the wall, but he managed to stop himself. He rubbed his hand over his face. He shouldn't have left her alone. Coming back from the Highlands he let her persuade him she wasn't in any further danger. His need to put some distance between them had left her vulnerable. She could have been the one lying unconscious on the table instead of Kate.

What if her system had been compromised from

the earlier poison? What if this second dose would have been fatal?

He started pacing the length of the room. He had to convince her to leave her clan and return to Wyoming. His clan would keep her safe, and he would find the bastard responsible.

Wait a minute. She said the tea was meant for her. She hadn't brewed it herself. He swung about. "Who gave you the tea?"

She swallowed and stepped forward. Her gaze darted to Celeste and back to him. "Davis…"

Celeste whimpered softly and peeked up at him from her drenched, swollen eyes.

Rage swamped him. He stalked forward. Bethany grabbed his arm. "Davis you cannot possibly believe Celeste had anything to with this!"

He glared down at Celeste while she burst into tears and hid her face in her hands. Did she really think her pathetic tears would sway him?

"Davis!" Bethany tugged on his arm. He spared her a glance. Her luminous eyes welled also with tears and pleaded with him to listen. She stepped between him and Celeste, placing her palms flat against his chest.

Damn it!

He closed his eyes and sighed. She stepped away from him and proceeded toward her sniveling friend. He grabbed her hand. "Stay away from her. You may think she's innocent, but I sure as hell am not betting your life on it."

Bethany frowned. "I trust her as I am sure you trust your friends. Trust my judgement, please."

He pinched the bridge of his nose. She knew damn well phrasing it that precise way would tie his hands.

The healer sauntered over and slapped his phone into his palm. Her gaze encompassed all of them, lingering on the sobbing Celeste. "That was an informative phone call. Ashley has done extensive tests since you were poisoned. I am going to analyze the samples I have to compare and determine if the same poison was used."

"But I didn't have the markings. Do you still think it could be the same?"

"Yes, but you weren't found for days after your poisoning. The marks could have faded enough not to be noticeable. From what Ashley has told me, it really is a miracle you survived. Let us hope Kate is as strong as you were."

The healer left the room. Bethany sat down next to Celeste and wrapped her in her arms. Celeste leaned into her and wailed.

Davis rolled his eyes. Women!

Chapter Sixteen

"Take me through it step by step. Starting with where you got the tea. Who made it?" Celeste blinked at him and looked at Bethany.

"Did you buy it at the shop around the corner?" Bethany squeezed Celeste's hand.

Celeste nodded and peeked up at him through her wet lashes. "It is where I always go."

"What shop?"

Bethany turned to him. "It's a small bakery which sells coffee, tea, etcetera. If you take a right outside the gates, it's about a block down on the corner. It's called, *Treats and More*."

"You said always. Is this a daily thing, weekly thing, what? Be more specific." Celeste kept glancing at Bethany.

Davis sighed. Before Bethany could respond, he held up a hand. "I want to hear it from her."

Bethany frowned at him and glanced at Celeste. "It's all right. Davis is simply trying to determine the sequence of events. He knows you aren't responsible."

He opened his mouth ready to say he knew no such thing, but Bethany glared at him.

"We take turns. My day is Monday, Kate's is Wednesday, and Bethany's is Friday. Tuesdays and Thursdays, we skip because Kate has a weekly department meeting on Tuesdays, and Bethany has one on Thursdays."

"Did you see who made the tea?"

"Umm…I guess so."

Davis stuffed his hands in his front pockets to resist the urge to strangle her. "Did you, or didn't you?"

"I'm not sure. I was looking at my phone."

"How many people were behind the counter when you gave your order?"

She bit her lip and stared at the ceiling. "Two…I think."

"Was there anyone else in the shop at the same time as you?"

Her brow puckered. "A few were sitting at the little round tables. A woman left as I walked in. And there were two men who came in after me. I think they were French." She peeked at Bethany. "They were cute. The tall one winked at me."

He silently counted to ten and strove for patience. "Was the tea out of your sight any time after the clerk handed it to you?"

"Well, no. I returned to the compound and carried it up to Bethany's department." She leaned back in her chair and then shot forward. "Wait. I stopped in my department first to put my purse in my drawer. I didn't want to lug it around." She rolled her eyes at Bethany. "I bought this new shampoo and conditioner the other day, and I keep forgetting to take it out of my purse. It weighs a ton."

"Was there anyone in your office at the time? Did you set the tea down anywhere? Could anyone have been close enough to slip something into the tea?"

She shook her head. "I don't think so. It was only a minute, and no one was around my desk. It was early.

People were just starting to arrive for work."

Either she was leaving something out, or it had to have happened at the shop. He would have to tread carefully to investigate a store on foreign soil. Hopefully there was video footage he could get access to. Tracing Celeste's path from the shop to Bethany and Kate was going to be challenging. He didn't want to involve local authorities. He would have to talk to the guards to see how they handled security issues with the locals. Not something he wanted to do. The more people involved, the more chance for mistakes. He had no one he trusted here. Not knowing who could be involved made him not want to share information, but he didn't see another option at the moment. He needed to find the one responsible. Celeste was the only viable suspect by her own admissions. Bethany wasn't about to accept her friend as a suspect, and he had to admit she didn't seem like the type to poison her friends. He wasn't absolving her from blame yet. She could be an Oscar worthy actress for all he knew. Could she have been working with Bryant all this time and now getting her revenge for his death or carrying out his plan to kill Bethany? Had they been secretly romantically involved with one another?

There were only more questions and not enough answers. One thing was for sure, he wasn't letting Bethany out of his sight again.

His phone vibrated, and he pulled it out to check the caller. It was Malcolm. Likely, Ashley had informed him of his phone call and the reason for it. He stepped away from the two sitting in the corner, but kept them in his sight, as he answered the call.

"Ashley told me a friend of Bethany's has been

poisoned, and it might be the same one Bryant used to poison Bethany?"

"Not sure if it's the same poison. There are some similarities in the symptoms. The healer is running some more tests based on what she learned from Ashley. That's not all, though. Bethany was the target. Her friend drank tea intended for Bethany."

"I see. Any leads?"

"Her other friend, Celeste, bought the tea from a shop off the compound. She claims it wasn't out of her sight since the shop."

"Do you suspect the friend?"

Bethany glanced up at him. With her exceptional hearing she could hear Malcolm's every word. He looked at Celeste. She was wiping her smeared makeup with a tissue. He didn't know if she could hear or not. She wasn't making any signs that she could. He didn't even know if or what she could shapeshift into. One more thing he needed to find out.

"Bethany doesn't." Malcolm would know it meant he was reserving judgement and hopefully it wouldn't upset Bethany too much.

Bethany frowned, but she didn't leap to her friend's defense or try to correct him. He hoped it meant she understood his stance on this.

"I know I don't have to warn you to tread carefully. You will have some help with this investigation. Aki is sending one of his guards, Kioshi, to assist you. His cover is the same as yours, council advisor."

He remembered Kioshi from the last time they visited the European compound. "You trust him?"

"I trust Aki, and Aki trusts him."

"Good enough for me. He knows everything?"

"Yes, I've been keeping Aki apprised of the situation. He had already decided to send Kioshi before I updated him on the latest. I was planning to call you today to let you know when Ashley informed me about the poisoning."

"When does he arrive?"

"Should be later today. I'll text you his information and relay yours to Aki to pass on to him."

"Okay, I'll get him up to speed when he arrives. It will be nice to have some backup."

"Good. Keep me informed. And Davis, if you need more backup call me immediately. You're not in this alone."

"Understood." Malcolm disconnected, and Davis slipped his phone back into his pocket.

He wasn't about to get all sappy, but he missed the connection of his clan. Knowing they always had his back was vital to his make up.

The healer entered from the side door. "I've run some further tests, and although I am still waiting on two other results, the comparisons to the poison given to Bethany and the one to Kate are strongly linked. I won't know if it's an exact match until all the tests are complete."

Bethany took a deep breath and stood. She had expected them to be similar, but why she wasn't completely sure.

"What does that mean for Kate?"

"I gave her the antidote for fallibar quickly. You were exposed longer to the poison, and therefore sickened more deeply. She hadn't ingested all the tea, plus she vomited some of the poison out of her system. It is my hope, and my professional opinion, Kate will recover more quickly. Now that I know some of the other ingredients I can watch for further toxicity and treat her accordingly."

Bethany walked over to Kate and stroked her arm. Her friend had to survive this. The guilt weighed heavily on her. Kate was lying there in her place.

"Right now, I need for you all to leave. Kate needs her rest."

Bethany was ready to protest. She intended to stay with Kate but staring into Elizabeth's dark eyes she knew there was no point in arguing. She nodded and faced Celeste and Davis.

Celeste stood several feet away from Davis, clearly waiting for direction from her. She knew in her heart her friend would never harm her. Despite the doubts her brother's betrayal had created, she would not believe Celeste intentionally put poison in her tea.

Davis stood feet apart and arms folded across his chest. An argument was coming from him. There was no doubt in her mind on that score. His faith in her friend or her own judgement wasn't as strong. He was going to argue guilty until proven innocent. He was back to being her self-appointed bodyguard.

Whoever was trying to kill her might not get a chance to finish the job. The stress of it all and the pain of the close proximity of a mate who didn't want her might be enough to finish her off.

Chapter Seventeen

"Lady Bethany, Lord Aaron requests your presence upstairs."

Bethany forced a smile for the guard, Ned. She was not in the mood to deal with her cousin this afternoon but ignoring him would not help his disposition any. Why couldn't he simply use the phone instead of sending one of the guards to fetch her? She sighed. Probably because she could ignore a phone call, but not a guard waiting to escort her to him.

Glancing up at Davis standing outside her cubicle with his back to the wall, she noticed his folded arm stance and aloof expression. The same position he'd been in all day. Kioshi, the guard from the Asian clan, had arrived yesterday morning. The two had shared long whispered conversations, and then Kioshi had disappeared while Davis continued as her silent shadow. He barely spoke to her except to protest her return to work this morning. He had been displeased with her decision to put it mildly. She had to return to work, though. It was either that or go insane dealing with the tenseness between them.

Standing, she shut down her computer and grabbed her purse. There was no telling how long Aaron would keep her. The topic of his conversation was a given—he wanted her support. She could not in good conscience provide it. Which meant this meeting could get ugly if he pushed the issue. She didn't think she would be able to put him off much longer. She had already put off meeting with him yesterday because she spent the day with Kate. The sight of her friend opening her eyes yesterday had filled her own with tears. Elizabeth had implied Kate should make a full recovery. A vast wave of relief had washed over Bethany with the prognosis. She had helped get her settled in at home, so she could spend the remainder of her recovery in comfort—surrounded by her own things. A guard was posted for her safety.

Bethany followed Ned into the elevator with Davis close behind them. How was she going to convince Aaron not to throw a fit at Davis' presence? She certainly doubted Davis would leave the two of them alone. He'd made his distrust and extreme disgust of her cousin well known.

Stepping off the elevator, she was prepared to step right, but Ned turned left. Surprised, she paused. Where was the meeting? Aaron's office and the conference room were both to the right.

Ned looked over his shoulder. "Lord Aaron has moved into your uncle's office."

"I see." No, she didn't. It was awfully presumptuous of him. How was Advisor Heyes going to feel about that? Did Aaron plan to barricade himself in there if he lost the vote? Sighing, she followed Ned to her uncle's former office.

Two guards stood outside the closed office door. She recognized them, but didn't recall their names. They both nodded at her and one opened the door. She started to stride through when the other guard held up his hand to Davis. "Only Lady Bethany may enter."

"Like hell. Where she goes, I go."

"Mr. Campbell is with me."

"Bethany, cease the theatrics and get in here. Your hulking Neanderthal will wait outside."

Before she could reply, Davis stepped forward between her and the door. Both guards stiffened. "No, I won't. You want to speak to her, you'll do it where I can keep an eye on you. And don't forget I'm here on the council's authority. You may have moved yourself into your uncle's office, but you have no power here."

Ned hissed a sharp intake of breath behind her, and she prayed a physical altercation wasn't imminent.

Leaning to the side slightly, she peeked at her cousin to gauge his reaction. She was at a loss on how to defuse the situation. His face was bright red, and she braced herself for an explosion.

"Leave the door ajar then if you can't bear for her to be out of your sight but make no mistake, I will rule the clan, and one of the first acts I will do is to see you permanently removed from the compound." Aaron stalked behind the desk and sat down.

Bethany placed her hand on Davis' forearm. "Please."

He glanced down at her and then back to her cousin. Giving a sharp nod, he angled to the side slightly giving her enough room to slip past him into the room. She glanced back at him after she passed. He stood in the open doorway sideways, so he could see inside the office and the hallway outside as well. Folding his arms across his chest, he glared in her cousin's direction before turning his gaze to each of the guards. For a moment she was worried they would interfere, but they quickly swung about and faced away from the office. Was her cousin aware he likely didn't have the guards' support should he try to enforce his rule?

Walking across the office and taking a seat in one of the chairs in front of the desk, she noticed little had changed since her uncle presided over the clan. The same antique gilded furniture, priceless paintings and sculptures filled the large room. Aaron may have moved in, but he hadn't changed much. The prized Oriental rug was missing from the room. Whispered rumors of her uncle's grisly murder had trickled down to her once she had returned to work. Her imagination could fill in the gaps. A beheading was the traditional method used for one Risharden to kill another. It was how her brother had killed Donald, and likely how he had killed their uncle as well.

Taking a fortifying breath, she squared her shoulders and stared at her cousin. "You wanted to see me?"

Aaron sat with the chair facing left leaving her to stare at his profile. His jaw was clenched tight, and his skin was a blotchy red. It saddened her, this man was her only remaining family. They had never been close. There had been little opportunity with her being raised mostly in the Highlands, but even when she had moved here full time, she had felt little kinship with him. He was always so angry, even as a younger man. Perhaps he was simply a product of his environment. He had been raised by her uncle after all, and he hadn't been an affectionate man. He had pitted Aaron and Bryant against one another for as long as she could remember. Feeling sympathy for his position would be easier if he exhibited a modicum of compassion and restraint.

"Were you aware your brother wasn't the only murderous traitor in the family?"

Sucking in a shocked breath, she clenched the arms of the chair.

"No, I don't suppose you were." He swiveled his chair to face her fully, crossed his legs, and placed his elbows on the arms of the chair. He tapped an index finger against his lips. "I have discovered some interesting tidbits about our family tree and our dear departed uncle. Would you like me to share them with you?"

Good Lord, what now? She could tell by the smirk on his face he was enjoying himself. No, she had no sympathy for him anymore.

"You are too young to remember much about your parents, let alone our grandparents as they died before you were even a thought. They were gone when I was but a child. What do you know about our grandfather?"

"Not much, I admit. He was the ruler of the clan. He had three children, Uncle Elsof, my mother, and your mother." She doubted he wanted to give her a history lesson.

"Do you know how he died?"

She tilted her head to the side and sighed loudly. "Old age?"

His eyes narrowed over her perceived sarcasm. "He drowned in the loch you call home."

No, she had not been aware of that.

"Where does the murderous traitor part come in?" Her cousin was drawing out his tale. The slight smirk on his face expressed his enjoyment of the situation. He relished this.

"Did you know our uncle kept journals?"

She inwardly sighed. A trait her brother had apparently shared. "No."

"Actually, neither did I until I moved into this office and found a stack of them hidden in the wall. Quite fascinating reading."

Glancing around the room, she wondered briefly which wall, but did it really matter? She really wished he'd get on with it, but at the same time dreaded hearing what awful family skeletons he was about to reveal. The glee on his face and in his voice were rather sickening. Didn't he realize this was also his family he was talking about?

"Dear Uncle Elsof was a bit of a braggart. He couldn't very well publicly brag about his deeds, so he wrote them down. For posterity's sake, I imagine." Aaron leaned forward and propped his elbows on the desk, pinning his gaze on her. "He killed his father in the loch and let everyone believe he died in his sleep." Giving an artless shrug, he leaned back. "He was ancient, so no one questioned him."

Closing her eyes, she wished the dainty chair had a higher back, so she could rest her head. It suddenly felt like it weighed too much for her neck to support. Her uncle had killed her grandfather?

"Would you like to know why?"

Opening her eyes, she stared at the lines the wooden planks made in the floor. Each one straight and narrow, no deviations, no cracks or grooves, or crazy lines. Unlike the path her family tree possessed. Those lines were bent, diseased, and downright rotten.

Aaron didn't bother waiting for her reply. "For the throne of course. You see our grandfather planned to announce his son was not his heir. He was choosing someone else to rule the clan. He foolishly told Uncle Elsof of his plans. Apparently thinking his son would calmly accept them. Dear old Uncle Elsof put an end to that." Aaron chuckled.

Nausea churned in her stomach. She wanted to leave the room, the building, the compound, the whole city. She was fed up with the violence and the sickening delight men took in killing one another for power. She wasn't naïve enough to believe some women didn't hunger for it as well, but men were enthralled by it.

Bethany gripped the arms of the chair, preparing to stand. Wait, who had her grandfather planned to name as heir? "He intended for one of his daughters to inherit the clan?"

Aaron outright laughed. "Don't be ridiculous. A woman cannot rule a clan." He clasped his hands together on top of the desk. "However, her husband could if named as a successor."

Bethany grasped her knees and locked her spine. She was damned if she would give him any more reason to gloat. She knew now why he called her in and didn't fight the issue of Davis staying within earshot. He wanted him to hear. He wanted everyone to hear. It was his father named to be the successor, and he would use this to cement his right to rule the clan.

"My father, not Uncle Elsof should have been ruler."

Pushing to her feet, she avoided eye contact with him. The sight of him was impossible to endure any longer. She had already decided she could not support him, but now she would oppose him with relish. She would support Advisor Heyes publicly. Aaron would not only perpetuate the twisted reign of the past but make it infinitely worse.

"Leaving so soon, dear cousin? But I have more news to share." Aaron stood and stalked around the desk to stand in front of her. "Uncle Elsof didn't stop his murderous tendencies with his father. Oh no, he made sure to eliminate any possibility of competition all together."

She stared at the floor in horror as the implications of his statement flashed through her mind.

"My parents and yours, dead at his hands. Quite the Machiavellian ruler our uncle was. I simply had no idea he had it in him."

Wrenching her gaze to his, she let the utter disgust and contempt show on her face. "He murdered our parents, and you sound as if you admire him. You are as depraved as he and my brother were. You don't deserve to rule. I will never support you."

Aaron seized her arm and dragged her up on her toes to snarl in her face. "I will rule, and you will show me your support!"

She wrenched her arm away as a furious growl sounded behind her. "Never!" She stumbled back as a blur rushed by her.

Catching herself against the wall, she gawked at the sight of Davis as a wolf straddling Aaron prostate on the floor. Davis snarled in his face.

Watching his jaws open, Bethany leaped forward. If he tore out Aaron's throat, it would mean war!

"Davis!"

She swung her gaze to the guards standing in the doorway. They made no motion to intervene, not that she could particularly blame them. A trail of shredded clothes was strewn across the floor. His fur stood on end around his thick neck. Saliva dripped from his snarling mouth.

Bethany stepped closer and held out her hand toward him. "Please, this isn't the way."

The wolf cocked its head slightly to meet her gaze before turning back to Aaron, who was gasping in horror on the floor. A long canine tooth appeared as he growled low before slowly backing off and standing between her and Aaron.

She couldn't resist delving her hand into the soft, thick fur of his coat. He leaned against her briefly before turning back into a man.

"Get him some clothes." Ned jumped to do her bidding as the two remaining guards stood in the doorway.

Davis stared down at Aaron. "Looks like he'll need a change of pants too."

Bethany glanced down to see the telltale wet spot on her cousin's pants and grimaced.

Chapter Eighteen

Davis paced the length of her living room while talking on the phone to Malcolm. They'd left Aaron shouting dire threats as spittle shot out of his mouth. Davis filled his clan leader in on the heinous acts of more members of her accursed family. She stopped listening at the recounting and started making herself some tea to soothe her nerves, but it only made her think of Kate and the poisoned tea she had drank. Pushing the tea back in the cupboard and turning off the stove, she wandered into her bedroom to stare out the window. Had Aaron been the one to assault her and try to poison her? Had he been working with Bryant all along or had he stumbled across her brother's scent blocker and poison like he found her uncle's journals? She hadn't thought her brother and Aaron had ever been close, but could it have been an act? Had they united against their uncle? Had Bryant known about their uncle's treachery?

Davis' light tread announced his presence before his reflection appeared in the window over her shoulder. "Malcolm is notifying the other council members of Aaron's claims and threats."

She turned to face him. "Even if what Aaron said is true, it's all based on my uncle's ramblings in a journal. It doesn't provide Aaron with a solid claim to rule the clan."

"That's basically what Malcolm said as well."

She nodded. Even if he wasn't guilty of colluding with Bryant, or the one trying to kill her, Aaron was too damaged to ever be allowed to rule the clan.

"Come back to my clan with me."

Bethany swung her head up. Her gaze collided with his. What?

"It's not safe for you here. My clan will protect you."

Ah, of course, he wanted her to go to protect her, not to claim her as his mate. She pivoted back to the window. What did it matter?

He stepped up behind her. "What's left for you here? More betrayal? My clan will welcome you."

"Why?"

"Why what?"

"Why would your clan welcome me? I am not only the sister of the man who murdered a clan member, but he also attempted to kill your leader and his mate. And then there is the rest of my horrible lineage. Why would they want me there? Why do you?"

Squeezing her shoulders, he pulled her back against his body. She closed her eyes. She wanted to turn and throw her arms around him.

"You know why."

She opened her eyes and met his gaze in the reflection.

"You're my mate." Joy and sadness rose within her at his words.

He dipped his head and trailed kisses down her neck. She tilted her head to provide him with more access. Davis touched her, and any thought of resistance fled. She wanted the pleasure she found within his arms—even if it was only one last time. His arms slipped around her waist, pressing her back flush to his front. She lifted her hands and covered his.

Davis couldn't resist the need to touch her any longer. She was his mate, and she had been endangered too many damn times. The rage had been simmering under the surface for days. When Aaron had dared to touch her, the only thought going through his mind was a need to protect what was his. He had barely stopped from ripping the bastard's throat out. Only she had stopped him. Her calming voice slipped past the fury and allowed reason to return. He needed her.

The taste of her soft skin urged him to devour her, but he wanted to savor every touch and taste. Her hands fluttered, hovering over his a moment before dropping back to clutch his thighs, as he raised his hands slowly up to cup her breasts. Two exquisite handfuls of perfection.

Her head dropped back against his shoulder. A soft, blonde tendril of hair tickled his nose. Bethany's eyes drifted closed on a soft exhale of breath. Her pale lashes fluttered over her ivory skin. An angel of such beauty, and she was his.

One hand continued to cherish her breasts while the other slipped down to unfasten her pants and slide inside. A bright pink blush bloomed on her pale cheeks as his fingers discovered the warm honey between her thighs. Her lips parted on a gasp, and he couldn't hold back the groan of arousal when the pleasure of her response washed over his fingers.

Swinging her up into his arms, he walked the short distance to the bed and laid her down. She helped remove her clothes and reclined back to watch him take off his own. He withdrew a condom from his pocket before dropping his jeans to the floor. He wasn't taking any further chances. Her eyes widened slightly when she spotted the condom. She blinked but said not a single word.

While Bethany welcomed him into her arms, he reveled in the feel of her skin against his. Kissing her deeply, his body demanded to join with hers. He couldn't hold back any longer. He donned the condom and returned to Bethany, sliding into her warmth inch by inch.

Their movements quickly became frantic with need. She cried out in release, and his orgasm hit him like a tsunami. Pleasure exploding in the base of his spine and rushing throughout his body.

He sank against her, momentarily unable to support his own weight. Sucking in a deep breath, he rolled over, taking her with him and tucking her against his side. Her hand lazily trailed over his chest.

The cool air swept over his sweat-dampened skin. He kissed her forehead and rolled to his feet. He walked into the bathroom to dispose of the condom and wash up. By the time he returned she had burrowed beneath the covers. Her gaze tracked him, but there was little emotion on her face for him to read. What was she thinking about? Would she go with him to his clan?

He climbed into the bed and pulled her back into his arms. She came easily, and he counted it as a good sign. He stroked her arm from the shoulder to her wrist and looped their fingers together on his chest.

"Should I make the arrangements for us to fly home?"

She stiffened slightly before she relaxed and

rubbed her cheek against his shoulder.

"I want to say yes."

"Then say yes."

She gazed into his eyes silently pleading with him to understand. "I cannot walk away and do nothing to prevent Aaron from claiming rule over my clan. If you were in my place, could you?"

He sighed. "If I were in your place, I would have killed him a long time ago."

The heat of her gaze burned him, but he closed his eyes instead. What did she want from him? Her decision was clear in her voice. He could admire her conviction and resent the hell out of it at the same time. She was making her choice. It wasn't him.

Chapter Nineteen

"What's that?"

Bethany glanced up at Davis peeking over her shoulder, and then back down to the vial she held in her hands. "I don't know. It fell out when I picked up the sweater."

Davis snatched it from her hands and opened the top. He sniffed it, and his face instantly hardened. As he swung about to leave the room, Bethany grabbed his arm.

"Wait, what is it?"

"The poison," he snapped.

Gasping, she glanced out the open doorway of Celeste's bedroom to the rest of her flat. Celeste and Kate were in the living area. Kate had insisted on getting out of her flat, so they had convinced her to come to Celeste's, the closest to hers. Kate had been chilled, so Bethany jumped up to get her a sweater from Celeste's drawer, while Celeste finished getting Kate some coffee. Her attempts at weaning herself off the brew long forgotten.

"Don't jump to conclusions! There has to be another explanation." She refused to believe her friend was guilty of trying to poison her. It was terrible enough her family was a pit of vipers. She couldn't accept her friend was as well. It just might break her.

"Fine, let's hear her excuses." He turned to go

147

again, and she tugged on his arm.

"Let me think for a minute. She couldn't have done it."

"There's no other scent here but hers. I know you don't want it to be true, but you can't keep denying the evidence stacking up against her. By her own admission no one else had access to the tea once she left the shop. Kioshi got ahold of the video at the shop, and there's nothing suspicious on the recording. The sample of the tea we took from the shop was normal. Logic suggests the poison was added somewhere between the shop and your department. Maybe that was the real reason she stopped back in her department before going to yours. To add the poison."

Bethany stared at his scowling face. He thought Celeste was guilty. She franticly gazed about the bedroom trying to come up with an alternative explanation. The white furniture with gold accents, canopy bed, dressing table all gave the room the princess feel her friend desired. Her friend had always been the one to believe in fairy tales and see the innate good in people. Could someone have taken advantage of that and tarnished her somehow? Convinced her to try to kill her? Why? For what possible reason did someone want her dead?

She shook her head. No, she refused to believe Celeste would intentionally harm either one of them.

"Did you find the sweater?"

Bethany swung her gaze to see Celeste standing in the doorway staring at them.

"What is that?" She stepped toward Davis and pointed to the vial gripped in his hand.

"You tell us. It was in your drawer."

Celeste frowned up at his scowling face. She glanced at the vial and then to Bethany. "I don't understand."

She stepped forward past Davis to approach Celeste, but Davis pivoted to block her. "No. You're not getting anywhere near her until we get some answers."

Celeste stepped back. "Bethany?"

Davis' anger was readily apparent and scaring Celeste. It would likely send her into a crying fit and get them nowhere.

"Stand down, Davis. You're frightening her."

"She should be terrified."

Celeste gasped and fled into the living area. Bethany let Davis see her exasperation before pushing her way around him to follow Celeste.

Kate sat up. Her tired blue gaze peered over the back of the couch. "What is going on now?"

Celeste stood by the kitchen with her wide eyes welling with tears.

Bethany approached slowly with her hand held out palm up. "Honey, don't get upset. I know there's a perfectly logical explanation for the vial of poison to be in your drawer."

"What!" Kate swung her gaze between Celeste and Bethany and landed on Davis.

Celeste burst into tears and wailed, "I don't know!"

Davis snorted behind her. Bethany sighed and started forward to comfort her friend. Davis clasped her shoulder, and she glared at him over her shoulder. "Stop."

He let go but dogged her steps as she walked over and wrapped her arms around Celeste.

149

Celeste's hiccupping sobs lessened, and Bethany guided her to a chair. She perched on the arm of the chair with her hand on Celeste's shoulder to soothe her. Celeste twisted the hem of her pink top in her fingers. Bethany and Kate shared a speaking glance. Neither of them believed Celeste capable of harming them.

Davis opened his mouth, probably to interrogate Celeste, but closed it when she adamantly shook her head. He rolled his eyes and stood silently with his arms folded across his chest.

This was not how she thought the day would go. She had planned to visit with her friends and then meet with Advisor Heyes to tell him of her support and warn him to be wary of Aaron and possible treachery. If she could be convinced her friends were okay and safe and Aaron would not rule the clan, then she could leave with a clear conscience and follow Davis home to his clan. She hoped once they were free of all the madness they would find a way to be with one another, as mates. His use of a condom had proven to her he wasn't thinking long term. The only reason to use a condom was to ensure she didn't conceive. Maybe if they were given the opportunity to focus on each other, that would change. They were mates. They each only had one shot. It had to be worth it to try and make it work. He had to see that didn't he?

But how could she leave now? Someone had been in her friend's flat planting evidence to frame her. It was the only possible explanation. Someone had used the scent blocker once again to hide their identity. They were all in danger, but she couldn't figure out why. What possible threat did she pose to anyone?

She caught Davis' gaze. "Someone is trying to

frame her. We need to discover who and why, as well as how."

Davis stared at Celeste for a long moment. Bethany shook her head. "She didn't do it."

He gazed back at her before nodding. "I'll trust your judgement. But she better fully cooperate in any investigation I deem fit. Which means her, and this apartment are going to be under full surveillance. If someone is framing her, I want undeniable proof. We need to catch this bastard once and for all."

Bethany rubbed Celeste's shoulder. Celeste peeked up and nodded. "I didn't do it," she whispered.

"I know, but we need to know who did. Who's had access to your flat?"

Kate handed Celeste a box of tissues. Celeste used one after another while biting her lip in thought.

"You, Kate, and my parents are the only ones with keys."

"Your parents are still in Italy, aren't they? Could someone have access to their key?"

Bethany glanced at Kate and nodded. "Good question. We all need to think about whether someone could have taken one of our keys or made a copy."

"You think someone broke into my parents' house and stole my key?"

"Your parents live in Italy?" Davis' question caused Celeste to tense. She swiftly shook her head but didn't raise her head or meet his gaze. "No, well, at least not all year. They spend the winter there and the rest of the year here in Scotland outside the city."

"Give me their address. I'll send Kioshi to check it out."

Kate leaned forward and grabbed a notepad and

pen from the coffee table. "I know it. I'll write it down for you." After writing it down, she handed him the paper. He nodded and ambled away to call Kioshi.

"Mine is on my key ring along with the keys to my flat and cottage, and a key to Kate's flat. I keep them in my purse. I don't see how anyone could have taken them, but I suppose anything is possible."

Kate snuggled back down on the couch. Her eyes were getting a bit droopy, a reminder her friend was still recovering. "Mine are hanging on the inside of the utility closet in my flat. Someone would have to know where I keep them. They're hidden behind a bunch of cleaning supplies."

Bethany gazed at Celeste. "Where do you keep your keys? Could anyone have had access to them?"

Celeste dabbed a tissue at her eyes. "I keep them in my purse. At work I put my purse in a drawer at my desk. I guess someone could have opened the drawer and taken my keys, but I would have noticed if I didn't have them to unlock my door."

Davis walked back over to join them. "Someone could have taken an impression of them to make a copy and then slipped them back into your purse."

Bethany sighed. "So, we are no closer to figuring out who could have done it or why."

"Not necessarily. Are there cameras trained on your desk?"

Celeste bit her lip. "I don't know. I never noticed if there were."

"There are cameras all over the building, so it very well could be." Kate closed her eyes. "I'm going to take a little nap. Feel free to figure it all out while I do. I really would like to know who I can kill for doing this to me."

Davis softly snorted. "Afraid you'll have to get in line on that one. The bastard is mine."

Bethany stood up. "You can argue who gets the right over killing them after we locate them. We need to get access to the security cameras."

"Yeah, been trying to do that for the time Celeste entered the building with the tea. Guards informed me it's already been looked at and nothing is there but refused to let me verify it myself. Kioshi was in the process of trying to hack into their system when I just sent him to Celeste's parents' place."

Bethany cringed. Did she really want to be privy to that kind of information? Unfortunately, there was no choice. She trusted Davis not to do anything damaging with the access if he did manage to get into the system. Besides, if Kioshi was able to hack into their security then obviously improvements were required. "Maybe they will be more forthcoming with me. It's worth a try."

Glancing down at Kate to see she had already drifted off to sleep, she shifted her attention to Celeste. "Will you be all right here while Davis and I go to the offices and see if we can view the video footage?"

Celeste nodded. Davis did a walkthrough of the flat checking windows. He gave Celeste his phone number before they left and instructed her to lock up behind them.

Bethany hugged her and followed Davis out of the flat. It made her smile because she interpreted it to mean he not only trusted her judgement where her friend was concerned, but he also made sure her friends were safe and felt protected.

As they approached the guards, Davis leaned down to whisper. "Okay, time to do your Lady Bethany bit."

Perplexed, she glanced over. "What bit?"

He softly chuckled. "The raised chin, pert little nose, and spine of steel bit where you pin those big beautiful eyes on them and will them into submission."

"I do no such thing."

"Uh huh, beneath that sweet exterior beats a heart of royal manipulation. You quietly maneuver everyone with smiles, calm reason, and gentle nudges."

"That is hardly flattering."

"Sure it is, makes everyone do what you want while still thinking you hung the moon."

Bethany frowned at him, and then quickly switched to a beaming smile as they reached the security desk. Her smile started to falter for a second when Davis chuckled behind her.

Damn it, she was not being manipulative—merely sincere and polite.

In the end, it didn't matter, although the guards allowed them to view the video from the day Celeste purchased the tea and of her department. There were no culprits caught on camera or suspects they could identify. There was no surveillance in the elevators, nor was there any that captured Celeste's desk. The only footage of her was her walking into the building, approaching the elevator, and then stepping off it in the design department and walking to the cubicle.

Trudging back to her flat, she kept running over the events in her head. Aaron was the only one with a current grudge against her now, since she had vowed to do everything she could to keep him from ruling the clan, but the incidents had happened prior to that so what reason could he have had to try to kill her then? Whoever was behind it had access to Bryant's scent blocker and poison so they either discovered it after his death or were working with him the entire time. Still, the motive eluded her. Bryant had wanted her dead because he believed she had tainted their precious bloodline by sleeping with Donald. A ridiculous reason in her mind, but the only one he had shared. Clearly, he had been insane.

She glanced at Davis beside her. His gaze vigilantly scanned their surroundings. Aaron despised Davis. He believed him and the other clans to be beneath him. Could that be his motive after all? Had Bryant and he united over their hatred? Could he be the one?

Although evil enough, did he have the intelligence and the patience to carry out a devious plan behind the scenes? Manipulating her brother, and then carrying out the deeds himself once he was dead?

Her instincts said no. Aaron had the tendency to crow his perceived achievements and erroneous opinions to one and all.

But her instincts had been wrong before.

Chapter Twenty

"It is definitely a man, below average in height, on the hefty side, but there is little to identify him beyond that."

Bethany studied the black and white grainy image Kioshi had gotten from the camera hidden inside Celeste's parents' house. It could be almost anyone. The photo only showed his back and the long dark coat he wore. Kioshi was right though, whoever it was, he was not a tall man.

She glanced up at Kioshi. His black eyes were full of intelligence and often lively humor. The laugh lines attested to that. His black hair was clipped short above his ears, and he was always dressed in an immaculate dark suit each time she'd encountered him. "I am sorry, but I have no idea who it could be."

Davis took the photograph from her to study it once again. His jean clad thigh rubbed against her leg where they sat next to one another on her couch. She wanted to lean against him, but he had been throwing out confusing signals once again. He'd kept his distance since last night. Granted they had been preoccupied with finding the poison and trying to track down the culprit, but was a little warmth out of the question?

"It's still a break. We know this man, whoever he is, is involved. Good catch finding the camera. This guy clearly didn't know it was there." Davis tossed the photo onto the table.

"Her parents had only recently had it installed. Celeste was unaware of it as well. She was surprised when I spoke to her this morning."

"That could be telling right there."

She turned her head to glare at Davis. "You are not trying to implicate Celeste again."

"No. Although, nothing disproves her involvement either. I was referring to her lack of knowledge. It could mean whoever this is gets his information from her. She's the link we need to focus on. She was the source of the tea, the poison was in her apartment, the keys at her parents' house." Davis looked at Kioshi. "You showed her and Kate the picture, right? They had no clue who it was?"

Kioshi nodded. "Kate studied the photograph intensely but was unable to guess at their identity. Celeste was horrified over a man breaking into her parents' home and barely glanced at it. She claimed to have no knowledge as well."

Bethany leaned forward. "Claimed?" She was getting sick and tired of everyone not believing her friend.

"Rest easy, little one. I too believe in her innocence."

Leaning back, she clasped her hands in her lap and nodded.

Davis glanced between the two of them. "We need to question her again. Find out who she talks to on a regular basis. See who could be drilling her for information. It's probably someone she is unaware of."

"Celeste is a social girl. She talks to everyone."

"Yes, but who has steered the conversation around

to the days she brings you tea, the fact her parents are away in Italy and they have a key to her apartment, most importantly who asks questions pertaining to you and your schedule or habits?"

"Is she dating anyone?"

Bethany stared at Kioshi. At first, she thought he was expressing a romantic interest, but then she realized he wanted to know if it could be how she was giving out information. "No, I don't believe so. She normally tells me when she goes on dates. Celeste is a romantic—she always believes the next guy she dates will be the one, her mate." She made sure to stare at Kioshi and not glance in Davis' direction at the word mate. "Anytime she has a date she gushes about the man. I think she would tell me if she was dating anyone."

"What if he asked her to keep it a secret for now? Would she?"

She pondered Davis' question. "No. I really don't think she would or could. She wouldn't see it as a betrayal to tell me or Kate."

"All right, let's start with questioning her about any men in her life. Not necessarily ones she may be dating, but all those she talks to on a regular basis. Especially the men where Bethany was brought up in the conversation."

Kioshi stood. "I will take care of this task."

Davis stood and shook Kioshi's hand. "Thank you. I want to finish installing the security cameras around this building, and I want to limit Bethany's exposure to the public until we get this handled."

Bethany sat quietly and resisted the urge to remind them both she was sitting right here. It was a useless endeavor anyway. She would, however, not be hiding in her flat until this person was caught. Davis would have to accept her stand on that decision.

Davis' phone buzzed while he walked Kioshi to the door. She recognized Ashley's sultry tones from the phone when he answered. A small twinge of jealousy reared its ugly head briefly before she squashed it down. She was his mate. Any past relationship he may have had was not her concern. *Much.*

Davis rolled his eyes and held the phone out. "Ash wants to talk to you."

"Um…okay." She took the phone, while he wandered off into her bedroom presumably to finish installing the surveillance equipment he'd been working on before Kioshi arrived.

"Hello'?"

"Hi, Bethany. I've been meaning to call and check on you, but I've been remiss in my duties as your healer."

"Oh, no, I am fine, fully recovered." Ashley had been the one to drag her back to the land of the living after Bryant's attempt to murder her. "Thanks to you, of course. I am forever in your debt."

"Good, I like chocolate. Lots and lots of chocolate."

Bethany laughed. "Duly noted."

"How's wolf boy treating you? Driving you crazy with his male attitude of superiority and he knows best routine?"

Grinning, she sat on the arm of the sofa. "There are definitely those moments, but he has his reasonable ones too."

"Do tell. I didn't know he was capable of those."

Ashley's sigh echoed over the connection. "Listen, I'm not the type to beat around the bush so here is my spiel. I've known him since forever. He's like another big brother to me. One slightly less cantankerous than my own. I know he's got his hang-ups, and don't we all, but he's loyal to the end. Sometimes too loyal, if that's even a possibility. His head is harder than cement. By that I mean he's beyond stubborn. When he gets something in his head it's impossible to shake it loose. Despite all that, he's got a heart of gold and whoever he gives it to is one lucky lady. So, don't stomp on it, or I'll have to come over there and rip yours out. Got it?"

Bethany sat frozen.

"You still there? Geez, did I just give my speech to dead air or did I scare you into silence?"

"Uh, no, I'm still here, and I heard you. You didn't scare me, but you may have momentarily shocked me into speechlessness."

"Okay then. I'm sure Davis will skewer me if and when he finds out, that is if my brother, Greer, doesn't beat him to it, but I had to say my peace. I didn't want the two of you screwing up something so precious and rare because of pride or stupidity. I figured you would be the more reasonable one. Was I wrong?"

"I sincerely hope not."

"Excellent, then my job is done. Feel free to call me anytime to ask for advice on how to deal with insufferable overbearing males, or just to vent about whatever lame brain move or dictate they came up with."

"Thank you. I believe I will take you up on that."

"See that you do. Bye, Bethany. Good luck."

Bethany stared at the silent phone. An interesting

conversation to say the least. A bit terrifying, too. Had Davis talked to Ashley about her? She didn't think so, and he didn't strike her as someone to gab about their feelings or relationships.

Davis strolled out of the bedroom. "I'm finished in there. I want to place some cameras on the roof." He stared at her. "What? You're looking at me funny." He scowled. "What did Ash say to you? She said she wanted to talk about your health."

"She did, well, she led with that anyway."

He folded his arms and sighed. "And?"

"The two of you are close, aren't you?"

"She's like my little sister, my pesky pain in the ass little sister. Why?"

Bethany stood and walked over to him. "Because she seems to know we're mates and wanted to give me advice on how to deal with you."

He stared down at her in surprise before closing his eyes and pinching the bridge of his nose. "God help us both then."

Chapter Twenty-One

Walking into the spiritual temple, Bethany gazed around the ceremonial area. It was a circular, cavernous, dark-wood paneled room with a raised dais in the center. Rows of removable wooden benches fanned out around the platform in sections. The benches could be rearranged to accommodate the different ceremonies or processions.

Davis had been a bit cranky since Ashley's phone call. After mumbling about her always sticking her nose into everyone's business and trying to meddle, he had started moaning over women and their desire to always discuss their feelings. She had stood quietly and waited for him to finish, silently hoping he would divulge some of those feelings. No luck there. He had snapped his mouth closed and dashed back to his surveillance equipment.

Advisor Heyes stood over by a series of tapestries depicting the War of the End on their home planet of Rishard. The vibrant colors had faded with age, but the gory depiction was still vivid. But then when had war ever not been full of violent death?

He talked softly to three clan elders. When he spotted her and Davis, he excused himself and rapidly approached them. "Lady Bethany, what a pleasure." He took her hands in his and nodded at Davis. "Mr. Campbell. What brings the two of you to the temple today? I, of course, heard of the tragic illness of your friend. Please rest assured, I will do everything within my power to locate the fiend responsible. I understand she is recovering at home? I would like to stop by and offer my counsel. It must have been quite the ordeal for her."

Bethany didn't think Kate would welcome the intrusion, as well intentioned it might be. "She still needs her rest. Perhaps in a few days she will feel up to the visit. There is another matter I would like to discuss." She lowered her voice. "I'd like to speak with you privately if I may?"

"Certainly. Why don't you wait in the meditation room? I will join you promptly. We are discussing the procedures for the vote next week, but we are almost finished."

Bethany nodded and walked across the room to a smaller square one which branched off the main room. Thick rugs were scattered across the floor, and cushioned benches lined the walls. A woman she recognized but didn't know well knelt on one of the rugs with her head bowed and eyes closed.

Davis stopped in the entrance and she glanced up at him. His phone vibrated. He looked at the caller id and then glanced around the room. "It's Malcolm. I should take this."

"Of course, but not in here." She tilted her head toward the woman, and he nodded. He surveyed the windowless room once again and stepped off to the side to answer the phone.

Walking into the room, she saw the private entrance door behind the large door to the ceremonial room was open. It allowed clan members to enter the private meditation room from the hall without going through the larger ceremonial room. She knew Davis hadn't seen the door and believed the main door to be the only entry point. She didn't rectify his perception because he was right around the corner and needed to take the phone call. She stepped over and glanced down the hallway which led to Advisor Heyes' private quarters, the children's spiritual classroom, storage areas, and the back entrance. Starting to shut the door, her gaze landed on the Advisor's door. It was slightly ajar. A noise emanated from the rooms.

Bethany glanced back at the woman still meditating and the open doorway to the ceremony room. Davis really wasn't going to be happy with her, but whoever made that noise could be gone by the time she got him. Besides, it was probably nothing. She stepped into the hallway and tilted her head. Someone was definitely in his quarters. Papers rustled together, and a quiet shuffle of shoes against the floor.

Sidling down the carpeted hallway she peeked into the room. The door wasn't open enough for her to see clearly so she pressed slightly on the wooden door and prayed it wouldn't squeak.

Luckily someone must keep it well oiled. It opened soundlessly, and she shifted to peer around the door. There was a small living area filled with plaid covered furniture trimmed in dark wood with a tiny kitchenette off to the side. A door, partially open, was directly across from this one. It appeared to be the Advisor's office. A wooden desk covered with papers and miscellaneous items was in view. The sounds were coming from behind the door where she couldn't see. She stepped fully into the living area and peered toward the office.

Biting her lip, she tiptoed closer. She really hoped she wasn't being colossally stupid and ended up getting herself killed. She just wanted a peek at whoever was in the adjoining room. This might be the only chance they had to identify the one behind everything.

As she inched closer a man with dark hair abruptly strode across her line of vision. She couldn't help it, she gasped.

The man whirled around and spotted her standing outside the doorway.

It was Edward Heyes, the Advisor's son!

Wait, he could be there legitimately. It was his father's home after all.

She opened her mouth to explain her presence, but the hostile glare he shot at her changed her mind. She lunged for the door.

Hearing a deep, furious growl behind her, she jerked her head over her shoulder and stared in horror.

He had transformed into a bear. A large, black, angry bear.

Bethany groped for the handle, a scream forming in her throat. Terror made her shake and stumble.

A massive paw hit her like a boulder—sending her flying through the air to land on the other side of the room. Another swipe of the paw slammed the door closed and slid the thick iron locks closed. She was locked inside with a bear clearly intent on killing her.

Shaking violently, Bethany finally managed to get on her feet. She didn't want to die. What chance did she have against its size and strength, or the length of those claws?

"Why?" she whispered. "I want to know why."

Maybe if she could get him to talk it would give Davis time to reach her. Plus, she really did want to know why. She couldn't recall ever even having a conversation with the man. What possible reason was there to want her dead?

He opened his jaws wide and let out a terrifying roar. His teeth, sharp points of death, on prominent display. She propped herself up against the wall and willed her knees to stop shaking and hold her up.

Just when she was certain he would lunge forward and tear her to pieces he gave a huge shake and transformed back to a man.

Bethany swallowed hard and took a deep breath. It was clear now he was the man in the video. Would he tell her why? Could she reason with him?

Edward glared at her as he stalked across the room and back again. "Why couldn't you simply die in America? But no, you had to survive and come back here to mess with all my carefully laid plans. I'm so close to achieving the end!"

Should she say anything? Would it encourage him or enrage him?

"Now how am I to explain this? I can hear the interfering American bellowing for you now. It won't be long until he sniffs you out."

Bethany struggled to listen over her pounding heart. She could hear Davis searching for her.

The pounding on the door announced his arrival before he yelled her name. Edward jumped across the room to slap a hand across her mouth. "One word and I'll end you now with a great deal of pain."

The hissed words in her ear and the smell of his fetid breath caused vomit to rise in her throat.

He dragged her into his father's office, shutting and locking the door. Bethany frantically searched the room for escape. Besides the desk on the back wall, the room was full of bookshelves filled to the brim with books and papers. Artifacts decorated the walls and littered the desk. Loose papers were stacked on a chair and on the floor. There was only one window, one tiny octagonal window high in the far wall. There was no escape.

He shoved her away from him and pulled at his hair.

Bethany inched her way around the desk to put some space and an obstacle in his path. "Why do you want me dead? What was your plan? Maybe I could help. You worked with my brother, didn't you?"

Edward glared at her. "Do you really take me for that much of a fool? Your brother was stupid and easily led. A whispered word here and there and he reacted predictably. He was so certain he was meant for greatness that a simple tale of royal bloodlines, actually true by the way, and he believed it was his fate to rule over the clan. I found it here in one of my father's old books. He relished the news, sought to rule over every clan, in fact. I prodded him just enough." He pounded on his massive, hairy chest. "I showed him how to embezzle from the company. I gave him the idea for the scent blocker, and even supplied him with the fallibar for the poison." He swiped his arm down in front of him. "He still managed to screw it all up. He was supposed to kill you off and your pathetic cousin, not just Elsof. Now I must clean up his mess by destroying that stupid book, so your cousin has no further ammunition in case I can't eliminate him. He surrounds himself with guards. And you and your stupid resiliency. Why couldn't you just die?"

Bethany kept him in her line of sight while sneaking frantic peeks around the desk and chair she had placed between them for anything she might use as a weapon. She desperately replayed Davis' short lesson in self-defense in her head. Watch the eyes and hit the vulnerable spots. Could she delay him long enough for Davis to reach her? "You were clearing the path for your father?"

He snorted. "Again, all it took was a few words in the right ears. The elders leapt at the idea to make my father the ruler. The inept fools believed it was their idea all along. I knew my father would be hesitant to accept, so I played devil's advocate telling him how much time and effort it would take because the clan was a mess and so needy. He, of course, only heard the clan needed him. Service to the clan above all." Rolling his eyes, he flung out his hand and sent an ancient stone tablet from their home planet crashing to the floor. He spit in its direction. "Once he's ruler, a simple accident will take him out of the picture, and I humbly and suitably grieving, will inherit the title. I will lead the clan to greatness."

Once again, treachery and death for power. Bethany shook her head. "And here I was walking right into your plan and helping it along, in fact. I planned to give your father my support. It's why I am here today. You did this for nothing."

"You lie! Why would you support him over your own cousin?"

"Because my cousin is not fit to rule the clan." She was fed up. She glared at him. Disdain and disgust spurred her words. "Neither are you. You've boxed yourself in. There's no escaping these quarters without everyone knowing what you have done."

Edward curled his lip. "I'll claim someone else was here. I came to visit my father and found you and him in here. Maybe you were conspiring all along. I got knocked out and when I came to, to my everlasting shock and horror, there you were, dead on the floor." He smiled. "All so simple, all it takes is a little planning. I befriended your little blonde friend. She sure likes to hear herself talk that one. She told me everything I needed to know about you and your routines. I injected the poison into the tea while she stood in the elevator *blethering* on to some idiot from sales. She never even noticed I was there. She's the perfect patsy, too. I'm sure I'll have no trouble whatsoever ensuring she takes the fall."

"Like you did with the poison in the tea and hiding it in her drawer?" His face registered surprise before he narrowed his eyes and scowled. "Yes, we know about that. Your plan didn't work very well that time, did it?"

He lunged toward her, transforming into a bear as he moved. Bethany leaped in the air, pushing off the desk as she tore her clothes and shifted into her owl form. She just had to hold on until Davis arrived.

A giant paw tipped with claws swiped at her as she flew to the high ceiling. The height wouldn't keep him at bay. He could reach her by climbing on the desk. There wasn't much room to maneuver, and it wouldn't be long before his claws shredded her wings.

A vicious yank pulled her toward him. Searing agony rent her asunder. He had one of her wings. Feathers spiraled to the ground drenched in blood.

With a surge of motion, she dove for his head.

She had claws too.

Her talons ripped through fur and gouged at his eyes.

Edward roared in pain and snapped at her with his teeth. Her wing tore as he ripped it again with his claws. She screeched and fell to the floor.

His head swung back and forth, and he swiped at the air in front of him with his bloody claws. Although now sightless, he was still deadly.

Bethany lurchingly hopped across the floor, desperately scrambling to put distance between them.

The sound of splintering wood and running feet echoed from the outer room. Would he get to her in time?

Claws raked down the side of her body. Black dots swam in her vision. She had to transform. As a human she might have a chance. As an owl she was paralyzed without the use of her wings.

Shifting into a human, she clenched her jaw at the scream building in her throat. Her right arm and leg were useless. Silence and time were the only weapons she had left.

As quietly as she could, she gritted her teeth and dragged herself toward the door with one arm and leg.

Papers and books went flying as he turned in circles blindly swiping at everything in his path.

Panting from exertion and pain, she propped herself up against the wall and struggled to reach the locks. A split second of silence had her glancing over her shoulder in terror. He stood frozen. Blood coursing down his snout, dripping onto the floor. He was listening for her.

With a last surge of adrenalin, she managed to unlock the door as claws sliced open her good leg.

The door slammed open, shoving her to the floor completely spent.

A blur of movement crossed her vision. Davis burst into the room, murderous rage etched on his face.

He wrenched a ceremonial sword off the wall and swung toward the bear's head as it sprang toward him with a roar.

The head fell with a sickening thump to the floor, and the body crashed next to it in a lifeless heap. Bethany's eyes and stomach rebelled at the grisly sight, but her body had stopped obeying her commands.

Davis fell to his knees in front of her, blessedly blocking her view. He held his arms out to his sides as if he was afraid to touch her.

"You're not going to yell at me, are you?" she whispered.

He stared at her for a split second with his mouth agape before giving a sharp nod. "Damn straight I am, as soon as you're not a bloody mess on the damn floor."

She opened her mouth to respond or at least give him a smile of reassurance, but it proved to be too much. The black dots covered her vision, and she knew no more.

Chapter Twenty-Two

The first thing she saw when she awoke was Davis asleep in the chair next to her. His soft snore made her smile. The sterile smell of the medical building twitched at her nose. Instead of the plain white walls of Elizabeth's exam room, the walls were a buttery yellow. A window looking out onto the same courtyard as the exam room occupied the center of one wall. It was a different angle than the window in the exam room, however. This was the recovery room. Glancing down, she started to laugh but the movement hurt too much. She looked like a mummy wrapped in white bandages practically from head to toe.

Davis sat up and opened his eyes, blinking at her. He rubbed a hand down his face. "You're awake."

"How long have I been out?"

He looked around the room and then pulled out his phone. "Just shy of twenty-four hours."

She raised her eyebrows. That long? "What's my prognosis?"

"The healer said you should heal, but it's going to take some time. You were pretty torn up. Even with our healing abilities, you might have some scarring."

She intended to query Elizabeth about exactly what it meant.

"Are you in pain?"

"A bit."

"Translation, you're in agony?"

Bethany frowned. "No, it hurts, but as long as I don't move, I can handle it."

Davis grimaced and abruptly rose from the chair. He walked over and swung open the door which led to Elizabeth's office and lab. "She's awake and in pain. Give her something."

Elizabeth appeared in the doorway. Pushing past him without a word, she approached Bethany with a smile. "Glad to see you awake. On a scale of one to ten how severe is the pain?"

"About an eight."

"That means it's a twelve. Give her something."

Elizabeth sighed. "Mr. Campbell, if you cannot control yourself, I will be forced to insist you leave."

Davis folded his arms across his chest and glared at her. "You can insist all you want, but I'm not going anywhere."

All right this was going to get out of hand. Bethany shifted to sit up and let out a gasp of pain. He leaped across the room to her side.

Elizabeth gently touched her shoulder. "I had to stitch you up. Try to limit your movement today. You should regenerate quickly, but the less pulling and stretching the better right now. Understood?"

Nodding, she lay back and closed her eyes.

"I'm going to give you something for the pain. It will make you a bit drowsy, but I think you need your rest, so it is a good side effect."

He hovered over her. Peeking up at him, she smiled slightly. "I'm fine."

"That's one of the stupidest comments out of your mouth. You are not fine."

She sighed. "I suppose now you're going to yell at me?"

He clenched and unclenched his fists against his thighs. "No, I'm not going to yell at you, but I would like to know what the hell were you thinking?"

"I heard someone in Advisor Heyes' quarters. I thought I could just get a look at whoever it was before they disappeared. It might have been our only lead."

Davis stared down at her in horror. He spun away from her and started to pace the room. Elizabeth returned and gave her a shot. She glanced at him a couple times before leaving.

He stopped abruptly and glared at her. "So let me get this straight. You knowingly left the meditation room by yourself without telling me when I was right outside the room because you heard someone in the Advisor's office and assumed it was the person trying to kill you? You deliberately put yourself in a killer's grasp?"

Bethany clamped her lips together. This was not going to go well. He was furious. She had expected him to be upset, but not quite this angry.

"What has been happening while I was asleep?"

Pinching the bridge of his nose, he took a deep breath. "Promise me you will never do something like this again."

"I can't do that." Before his appalled expression could lead to an explosion, she rushed on. "Would you have done any differently? If you thought it was our only chance to catch the one responsible and end this nightmare? I don't intend to seek out danger, not by a long shot. I would happily never experience any violence the rest of my lifetime. However, if someone I care about is in danger or has been hurt because some crazy person was after me, then yes, I will do everything in my power to stop them."

The outer door opened and Kioshi, Kate, and Celeste hovered in the doorway. Davis glared at the lot of them, and then strode across the room to stand by the window. Kioshi nodded at her before proceeding to go stand by Davis.

Kate and Celeste approached and stood on either side of the bed. Celeste predictably burst into tears. Kate rolled her eyes and frowned down at her. Her friend's coloring had improved remarkably. She was even wearing a bit of lip gloss. Proof she was healing from her own ordeal. She tossed her head in Davis' direction. "Your bodyguard over there hasn't let us in to see you. How are holding up?"

Bethany smiled wanly at her. "I'm alive, and this nightmare is finally over."

Kate nodded and glanced at Davis and Kioshi. "Your cousin is demanding an immediate vote. He claims Advisor Heyes was aware of his son's crimes and was in fact the mastermind behind the entire plan all along."

Bethany sighed. Of course, he was. Aaron was bound to take full advantage of the situation. Could she still support the Advisor after what his son had done? Yes, she could. He was still an infinitely wiser choice than Aaron. Besides, he couldn't be held responsible for his son's perfidy. She certainly didn't want to be held accountable for her family's crimes.

"Has Advisor Heyes said anything?" The poor man must be devastated.

Davis stepped closer. "The last time I saw him he

was bawling over his son's body. You need your rest."

She winced. Celeste sniffled. "I can't believe Eddie could do all that. He was always so sweet."

"Did he say anything to you?"

She looked at Kate. "He confessed to manipulating Bryant into embezzling money, and to killing Elsof and trying to kill me. Bryant was supposed to kill Aaron as well. He wanted the way cleared for his father to rule the clan and then he would succeed him." She angled her head toward Celeste. "I'm sorry, Celeste, but he was using you just like he used everyone."

"I feel so stupid." Celeste held the tissue to her mouth.

"There's nothing wrong with seeing the good in people. It's one of the things that makes you so special. Don't take on the burden of his crimes. You did nothing wrong."

Kate walked around the bed and put her arms around a crying Celeste. "Bethany's right. You seeing the world through your rainbow glasses drives me crazy at times, but I wouldn't alter a thing."

Smiling at her friends, she struggled to keep her eyes open. The pain medication had taken effect.

Davis stepped up to the side of the bed. "You all need to leave. She has to rest."

After saying their goodbyes, her friends and Kioshi left. She looked at Davis. "Well?"

"Well what?"

"I saw you and Kioshi whispering over there. What's going on?"

He sighed. "He has been keeping me abreast of the investigation into Edward. The guards searched his apartment and office at the company. They found duplicate files on his home computer of everyone in the clan. He also had financials he should not have had access to."

"Is that all? What about the poison? Scent blocker?"

"No trace of the poison, yet, but they came across the scent blocker. They didn't know what it was. Kioshi has relieved them of it with them none the wiser. The less people who know about it the better."

She nodded sleepily.

"Get some sleep."

She closed her eyes. Just for a moment or two.

Her breaths grew deeper as she drifted off. She looked so damn fragile and vulnerable. The bastard had almost killed her. How she had held him off so long he couldn't fathom. She had not only survived but blinded him in the process and managed to get the door open. So much bravery in such a tiny package.

He had failed to protect his mate. The guilt chaffed. He understood the horror and rage Malcolm had experienced when Elsie had been kidnapped. How did he not keep her locked up in the house and away from any possible danger?

Shaking his head, he dropped down in the chair beside her. Now that Edward was caught, and dead would she return to his clan with him? Or would she have some other excuse to stay? He needed to go home and be surrounded by his clan. He wanted to take his mate home where he knew his clan would always have his back to protect her.

Chapter Twenty-Three

The clouds were thick and gray. Rain was imminent. Looking around at her clan gathered in the square to hear what Advisor Heyes had to say, she wondered and fretted over their future. She had insisted on attending when she heard he planned to address the clan. Davis and Elizabeth had consented as long as she stayed in the vile contraption of a wheel chair at the back of the square—away from the crowd.

Davis stood on one side of her and Elizabeth on the other. Three days had passed since the attack, and she was on the mend. She felt perfectly capable of returning to her flat, but these two acted like she was crazy when she suggested doing so.

Aaron, flanked by two guards, stepped out of the office building and approached the podium which had been set up for the speech. He stopped at the side and faced the crowd with a satisfied sneer firmly planted on his face. The rumor was Advisor Heyes would step down and officially remove himself from the running to rule the clan which would leave Aaron unopposed. By the expression on his face, she gathered he felt the same.

Advisor Heyes approached from the tree-lined path leading to the temple at the corner of the square. He wore his customary purple robe with his hands clasped in front of him. He stepped up to the podium and gazed out over the crowd. His face was pale and drawn. His hair and goatee were streaked with more white than she remembered. His son's treachery and death had aged him considerably in just a few days.

The crowd grew silent as anticipation held them all in his grasp. Soon the only sounds were the distant city sounds from outside the compound.

"It is with a heavy heart and stricken soul that I stand before you today." He cleared his throat. "My fellow clan members, as many of you are aware my son committed heinous atrocities against members of this clan and orchestrated acts to irrevocably damage the clan itself. He paid for these crimes with his life." His voice broke, and he glanced down at the podium for a moment. "I can no longer in good conscience seek to guide the clan to a future I can only pray is achievable. Therefore, I formally remove myself from the vote to rule the clan." Murmurings multiplied throughout the crowd. "Our future leader must have not only the strength to rule, but the wisdom and honor as well. We are at a desperate point in time. Our people must rise to meet the challenges we face, not with violence and selfish greed, but with a clear vision of what the future can hold for all of us."

Aaron was scowling at the Advisor. Bethany could see his patience was wearing thin, and he had to know the veiled insult had been directed at him. "It is my sincere hope you choose a leader who has demonstrated not only unimaginable bravery and strength of will but has always shown a clear head and deeply honorable heart. I therefore nominate Lady Bethany to lead the clan."

Gasps and surprised whispers echoed all over the

square. Shock held her immobile. Dozens of gazes were trained on her. Aaron's face was turning purple, and he glared at her with rage. As if she had anything to do with this!

Advisor Heyes was making his way toward her. The crowd parted for him, and she had the desperate urge to flee. What could he possibly be thinking? Had grief over his son driven him insane? She couldn't be the clan leader. A woman had never ruled over the clan.

He stopped before her. "Lady Bethany, I apologize for springing this on you unaware. I had wanted to speak to you privately before this, but Mr. Campbell forbade it."

They both glanced at Davis. He stared straight ahead. His face was completely emotionless. What on Earth was he thinking?

"My deepest apologies for what my son did to you." He took a deep, stuttering breath.

She stretched out her uninjured arm and clasped his hand. "Advisor Heyes, you owe me no apology. I am so sorry for your loss. Despite his transgressions, he was still your son, and I know you are grieving."

Clearing his throat, he nodded and gave a slight bow. She could see the tears glistening in his eyes.

"Thank you. Your kindness and compassion are part of the very reason why you will make an excellent leader."

She sucked in a breath. "Advisor Heyes—"

He held up a hand. "Please, before you say anything, think on it for the remainder of the day at least."

Glancing at over a hundred of her people watching and listening to their every word, she nodded. He turned and left, walking back toward the temple. She looked over the crowd to spot her cousin hoping he wasn't going to force a confrontation, but he had disappeared. That couldn't be a good sign.

"I'd like to go back inside."

Davis maneuvered her chair back into the building and into the room she was staying in. She stood on her own and climbed into the bed covered in royal blue sheets. She was going to insist on returning to her flat today, but after the crowd dispersed. The last thing she wanted to do was answer questions from a stunned clan. She was just as surprised as they must be, and she had no clue how to handle it all.

"I feel the need to express what an admirable clan leader I believe you would make and hope you carefully consider Advisor Heyes' nomination."

Elizabeth strolled out of the room. Bethany's jaw dropped, and she snapped it closed. Had everyone gone crazy?

Leaning back against the pillows, she looked at Davis staring out the window. "You are awfully quiet. Did he tell you what he planned?"

Davis turned and leaned against the wall with his hands in his front pockets. "No. I had assumed he wanted to speak to you about his son. I wanted you to heal first."

She nodded. "Crazy, right?" She smiled expecting a smile in return, but he continued to gaze at her solemnly.

"Actually, I think you would make a great ruler."

"What?" Was she dreaming? She must be still unconscious and having a drug-induced hallucination.

"Everything he said was true. You are the perfect

choice to lead your clan. The people love you, because you genuinely care about them and want what is best for the entire clan—not just the self-serving needs of the few. You also don't crave the power, which is why you won't abuse it. You know it's a responsibility not a prize."

Tears threatened, and she swallowed. "I don't know what to say."

He shrugged. "There's really nothing to say. It's a logical choice. Besides, you could never let Aaron rule the clan, not if you could prevent him."

"Even if I do choose to make a claim, the clan might still vote for Aaron. He's a man after all. I don't know how many of the clan are ready to accept a woman as a leader."

"I think you'll be surprised. You never know until you try."

"So, you think I should do it? What about his claims his father was the rightful ruler, and thereby him?"

"As you said, it's what he claims. Where's the proof? He hasn't provided any. If he had any don't you think he'd be showing it to everyone? Doesn't matter anyway, it's just hearsay, nothing official."

"You didn't answer whether you think I should do it or not." Did he no longer want her to return to his clan? Was it simply to protect her from Edward? Now that the threat was removed, did he no longer plan to claim her as his mate? Did he want her to accept the nomination, so he could leave with a clear conscience?

"The choice is yours."

Chapter Twenty-Four

Davis hung his head and let the hot water beat down on his shoulders. He'd left Bethany at the healer's with Kate and Celeste visiting her, and Kioshi standing guard. He had been in desperate need of a shower and change of clothes, so he had returned to his suite. He didn't think Aaron would dare try anything, but the coward had to be scrambling after the announcement.

He'd known as soon as the advisor started describing the qualities needed in a leader who he was going to say. Even before he said her name, he'd known he'd lost her.

Bethany would choose her clan.

Davis didn't expect anything else. He slapped off the water and grabbed the towel he had hung over the glass doors. There was no way he could ask her to turn her back on her entire clan and leave it in the hands of Aaron. He wasn't that selfish.

Stepping out of the shower, he wrapped the towel around his waist and wandered into the bedroom. Glancing at the clock on the nightstand, he calculated the time difference between here and Wyoming. Malcolm should be awake. He needed to fill him in and tell him he would be home soon.

****

"Please tell me you haven't uncovered evidence of another accomplice and they're still on the loose."

Davis snorted. "No, Heyes was the last one. It's all wrapped up nice and tidy."

"Is it? Then what is it I hear in your voice?"

Sighing, he wiped a hand through his damp hair. "Your mate making you want to discuss feelings now?"

Malcolm chuckled. "As a matter of fact, we've had a few conversations on the subject. So why don't you tell me what's going on."

"Advisor Heyes gave a speech in front of the whole clan and nominated Bethany as ruler."

There was only a brief stretch of silence. "She's a sound choice."

"Yeah, I know."

"What does she have to say about the nomination?"

"She was shocked as hell, but I think she'll come around and see it's the logical step for her to take."

"Do you think her cousin is going to be a problem?"

"I plan to stick around long enough to see that he isn't."

"I see."

Davis frowned and glanced at the phone. "What's that supposed to mean? What exactly do you see?"

Malcolm sighed. "She's your mate."

"No shit. I know damn well she's my mate, but what kind of selfish bastard do you take me for? I can't stand in the way of her leading her clan. I'll make sure she is safe and then I'll get the hell out of the way."

"You haven't bonded with her."

Bonded mates linked their spirits together. It gave them a deep connection even death was often unable to sever. Bonded mates rarely survived long without the other. His parents sure hadn't, not even to raise him.

"Been a little busy, and she hadn't made her decision to come home with me. It's a damn good thing we didn't, seeing as we'll be living on different continents."

"And you're okay with that?"

"Again, not much choice here, Malcolm."

"I think you do have a choice. You know we'll always be your clan, your family. Distance isn't going to alter that. But Bethany is your mate. Can you really live without her? Do you want to?"

Davis sat on the bed. The thought of living without her made his chest hurt. When he had seen her lying bloody on the floor and believed she might die, he hadn't wanted to go on. Tears stung his eyes, and he stared at the ceiling.

"You need to talk to her. There are always options and compromises to make."

"You're saying stay here."

"I'm saying you need to be wherever she is, so if it's there, yes. Besides, wasn't it you who was talking my ear off about the security nightmare over there and all the changes that needed to be made? I happen to know just the guy to be put in charge of all that. Sound familiar?"

"Damn, Malcolm, I thought you liked me. That's one giant headache you're suggesting I take on."

"Admit it, your palms itch to whip that place into shape."

He was right. If his mate was going to be staying here, then he would have to ensure her safety. The current state of the clan's security was insufficient in the extreme. They would need more guards, more surveillance, and a whole list of procedures. First item on the list would be to explore those tunnels and secure them.

A chuckle interrupted his thoughts. "Already making plans, aren't you?"

Davis shook his head. "Thanks Malcolm."

"Anytime, and I meant what I said. We're always going to be your family."

"There you go with those feelings again. What's she done to you?"

Malcolm laughed. "Tell Bethany I can't wait to welcome her to the council and the family."

Davis hung up the phone and ran a hand over his face. Well, hell, that phone call certainly hadn't gone the way he thought it would.

****

Bethany limped down the hallway as quickly as her aching body would allow. She had slipped out of the healer's building after telling Kate and Celeste she needed to use the bathroom. They had started following her to help until she insisted on going alone. Why did everyone feel the need to treat her like an invalid? She sighed. That was unfair. They were simply concerned and wanted to help in any way they could.

After evading them, she had snuck into Elizabeth's quarters and climbed out a window to avoid Kioshi and her friends. She would apologize to them later, but she needed to talk to Davis.

His withdrawn attitude frightened her. She grew tired of waiting for him to claim her as his mate.

She was claiming him.

The clan would survive without her. They had to be smart enough not to vote for Aaron. If they weren't, well, she would contemplate the dire outcome if it occurred. Right now, she needed to find Davis before he did something stupid like go home to Wyoming without her. And if he already had, well then, she would get on a plane and follow him.

A door opened down the hall, and she stiffened. She had already been waylaid a dozen times on the way over here by clan members giving her their support. She appreciated it, she really did, but she needed to see Davis.

Reaching the door to his suite she was suddenly afraid. What if he turned her down? What if he simply didn't want her?

Straightening her shoulder, she knocked on the door. She would just have to change his mind.

The door opened, and every thought flew out of her head. He stood before her with nothing but a white towel wrapped around his waist. The sight of his long, leanly muscled body made her throat run dry.

He looked beyond her down the hall. "Where the hell is Kioshi? Are you seriously telling me you walked all the way over here, and by yourself? You need a damn keeper, woman!"

"Are you applying for the job?"

One side of his mouth quirked up. "Somebody has to do it. It might as well be me."

Not exactly a declaration of undying love, but it was a start. "Good. When do we leave for Wyoming?" She marched past him into the suite. She wasn't about to let him know but she was more than a bit sore and tired from her escape out the window and trek across the compound.

"Wyoming?"

She glanced over her shoulder on the way to the couch. "To your clan. We're going to live there, aren't we?" Did he want to go somewhere else instead? She couldn't imagine him wanting to live away from his clan.

Davis' phone buzzed, and he glanced down at it in his hand. He sighed. "Hold that thought. It's Kioshi. I want to know what the hell he was thinking."

"Don't be hard on him. I snuck out."

He glared at her while he answered the phone. Kioshi spoke rapidly, informing him she was missing. "She's here." She heard Kioshi apologize profusely. "I can hardly blame you since she's done the same to me."

She winced as he disconnected the call.

"We really need to have a long discussion about this tendency you have to slip away from those trying to protect you."

"Mmhmm."

Davis sighed and sat on the table in front of her and took her hands in his. He gently rubbed his thumbs over the tops of her hands. "We're not going to Wyoming. Although it pleases me to no end that you were willing to go."

"I don't understand. Where are we going?"

"Nowhere. We're staying here. Your clan needs you, and truth to be told it needs me, too. The security here gives me a migraine."

"You want to live here and be in charge of security?"

"Once you're elected to rule the clan, I figure I'm a shoe in for the job."

Tears blinded her. "You're assuming an awful lot."

"You don't think I'd be good at the job?"

She wiped the tears off her cheek. "I meant that I would win the vote. You would be wonderful in the position."

He cupped her cheek and wiped the tears with his thumb. "You're the only one for the job. Why are you crying?"

"Because I'm happy."

He chuckled. "I'm never going to understand women."

"You only need to understand one."

He grinned. "You're right, and that is a full-time job."

She gave him a watery smile. "I was afraid you were leaving without me."

His grin faded, and he swallowed hard. "I thought it was the right thing to do, but a friend helped me to realize you're my home. You're my mate. I love you."

She leaned forward to throw her arms around his neck. "I love you so much."

His arms slid around her and gently squeezed, careful to avoid her injuries still healing. "As soon as you're well enough I want us to bond."

"I'm well enough right now."

He chuckled and pulled back slightly to kiss her softly, tenderly on the lips. "No, you're not. I can see you're in pain even though you're trying to hide it. Believe me I'm eager to make love to you and seal our bond, but the last thing I want is to cause you any more pain."

Biting her lip, she had to admit he was right. There was nothing in the world she wanted more than to bond with this man, but she didn't want to mar the special occasion because of her injuries. Thank goodness she healed fast.

Chapter Twenty-Five

His strong hand gently gripped and lifted her thigh to wrap around his naked hip. The tempered strength of this man, her man, made her feel cherished. He had insisted on waiting five anguishing days before making love to her again in order to allow her to fully heal. Despite her best efforts to seduce him beforehand, he had remained steadfast. Now, finally, they would become bonded mates, intertwining their souls and linking them together forever.

Each bonded mate's pairing varied, and she was curious how theirs would manifest. Their emotional connection would deepen, experiencing one another's feelings as if they were their own. An intuition often formed, warning if a bonded mate was in danger or distress. Some even experienced a telepathic link with their mates, giving them the ability to communicate with one another without the use of vocalized speech. If one died, the other would often follow, and with some mates it was instant. She'd heard of a mate dying the instant her mate had, although a continent away.

Davis' lips left a scorching path up her arched neck to reclaim her lips. Her tongue caressed and cajoled his into a fierce dance. A faint sweet taste of butterscotch laced his tongue. She delved her fingers through the thick strands of hair over his ears. The silky texture caressed her fingertips.

Careful to keep the majority of his weight off her, he leaned on his elbow and fondled her eager flesh with his free hand. Bethany hooked both legs around him to pull him closer. She desired the weight of him upon her body. He needed to know she wasn't a delicate, injured flower.

The groan he emitted prompted a burst of pleasure in her core. Cradling him between her thighs, she felt the heated length of him parting her folds with every movement. Rapture surged within her.

"Davis, now, please."

Leaning slightly away, he reached between them and entered her in a single stroke. They stared into each other's eyes as the waves of bliss intensified.

A shocked gasp escaped her. A pervading warmth wrapped around her like a gentle hug. The essence of her soul extended toward his. A golden glow surrounded them both. She opened herself completely to him. Sparkling lights teased the edges of her vision as she felt the bond snap into place.

A lightning strike of ecstasy shot through her entire body. She arched and cried out as the monumental orgasm crashed over her.

Davis clutched her tightly in his arms. Each pulsation of his completion sent another spiral of pleasure through her.

His warm breath bathed her cheek as he rose above her. She traced each of his eyebrows with her fingertip, then followed the path of his nose down to his full lips. He kissed the tip of her finger.

Tears welled in her eyes and overflowed. She could feel him deep in her heart. Their love encircled them both, like a living breathing entity. It was magical.

Davis stared into the face of his mate and marveled at the beauty shining from her. He placed a tender kiss over each tear on her cheek. Her love was pure and almost blinding. It bathed his entire essence.

He finally understood the devastation his mother must have felt at the loss of his father, her bonded mate. To have to go on without Bethany would cripple him. She was a part of him now. One existed for the other.

Cuddling in each other's arms, they each reveled in their new-found bond.

Bethany glanced around at the muted gray color pallet of the guest suite's bedroom. It was spacious and well appointed, but rather sterile. She preferred her own cozy bedroom in her flat or the cottage.

"I can practically feel the wheels turning in your head. What are you thinking? Besides how amazing your mate is that is."

Grinning up at him, she lowered her head to place a kiss on his chest. "You are amazing."

"But?"

"No buts. It just occurred to me that this room is nice, but I prefer my own. Although, I wouldn't mind this bed." She glanced around the width and length of the bed to see plenty of room remained even with the two of them reclining in the center.

He chuckled and kissed her forehead. "I definitely prefer the bed. And we do need to discuss our living arrangements."

"What do you mean?"

"I mean your apartment is sweet, like you, but it's too bloody small."

"I suppose giving up my cozy flat is a small price to pay in exchange for having you here."

"Besides, isn't there a suite up here or a penthouse for the leader of the clan?"

"Again, getting a little ahead of ourselves here, but there isn't a flat in this building designated for the leader. Although if you have your heart set on it, I'm sure we could arrange something."

"Where did Elsof live?"

"In the royal palace," she mumbled.

Davis peered down at her. "Excuse me?"

"It's what he insisted on calling it." She rolled her eyes. "My uncle spent many of his formative years in England. Gossip states he was rather a hellion. Perhaps it is the reason why his father, my grandfather, planned to disinherit him, or maybe he suspected the evil he was capable of. I guess we'll never know. Anyway, he compared himself to the royal family a great deal. When he became leader, he completely renovated the clan leader's residence, adding on two enormous wings on either side of the original structure. It sits on a small rise overlooking the river."

"That's a single home? I thought it was another apartment building."

"Ostentatious, I know. His tastes were extravagant."

"He lived there alone?"

"Other than some staff, yes. He preferred his privacy."

"So, we'd be living in a palace, huh?"

Bethany looked up at his smiling countenance. He appeared quite pleased with the thought. "You like that do you?"

"Who doesn't like the idea of living in a palace?"

"Well the vote hasn't happened yet, so the whole

discussion is moot."

"Are you nervous about tomorrow?"

She sighed. Was she? The election was tomorrow. She had accepted the entreaty to run against her cousin to rule the clan. He had been predictably furious. After the initial outbursts, he had become less visible, however. Perhaps she should be concerned about what he was up to, but she couldn't dredge up the slightest anxiety. What would be, would be.

"No, I'm not."

"Confident you'll win, are you? I like it. Confidence is sexy." He nibbled on her neck and growled.

Laughing, she returned his kisses before slipping back down along his side and rested her head on his chest. "It's not that. I'm too happy to worry what tomorrow will bring. I want to savor how I feel right now in this moment. I know whatever happens tomorrow I will be fine with you by my side."

"Good, because I'm never going to leave it. I thought I couldn't exist without my clan, but it's you I can't exist without."

Bethany sniffled and playfully swatted at his chest. "I'm turning into a watering pot."

"That's okay, with our bond I can tell they're happy tears, so I know what to do with those."

"Oh? What is that?"

"This!"

Davis rolled her beneath him and kissed her until they were both panting for breath and any tears were long forgotten.

Epilogue

The strident sound of cheering overwhelmed Bethany as she gazed out over her clan gathered once again in the square—only this time they were welcoming her as their new ruler. The vote had been held, and she had won by a landslide. Aaron had left in the middle of the night, taking some family heirlooms from Elsof's, now her, office with him.

Davis had been right, Aaron's claims his father had been intended to succeed their grandfather had been a lie. Her father was the one who had been named. Kioshi had found Elsof's journals in Aaron's flat. She tried not to think too hard about the breaking and entering he had done to find them. She had confronted Aaron with the truth but had refrained from airing it to the clan. In the end it hadn't mattered. The clan had chosen her without the knowledge.

She had expected Aaron to cause trouble, but perhaps he had seen the futility in continuing to claim rule over the clan. Davis was keeping tabs on him to be safe. He had fled to the Canary Islands. That was fine with her. As long as he posed no threat to her clan, he could live out his life in peace. Preferably far away from her and those she loved.

Members of Davis' clan had arrived this morning to show their support and welcome her to the family. Malcolm and his mate, Elsie, had surprised her the most. Elsie was beautiful. She had expected no less, but she hadn't anticipated the comradery between her and her clan or the ease with which she blended in with the Risharden as a whole. It boded well for their race on many levels if a human could not only adapt but be welcomed. Finding one's mate may have become an easier endeavor with their example leading the way. Malcolm appeared a different man than the one she remembered. A lightness surrounded him which hadn't been there before. It appeared as if his mate had freed him from some heavy burdens. Ashley was as stunningly beautiful as she remembered in an emerald green form fitting dress—with her wild mane of hair cascading down her back. She, Kate, and Celeste had instantly hit it off. She feared her friends might be making plans to visit the North American clan to look for mates. Ashley's brother, Greer, stoically glared at everyone. Davis had been shocked by his friends' arrival, and she knew deeply touched.

Aki, the leader of the Asian clan, had arrived with a small entourage of guards as well to witness the ceremony and welcome her as a new member to the council. Kioshi would be returning with him to his own clan. She would miss his presence. She knew Davis would be consulting him in the future as he revamped the security on the compound. The two of them had already had many animated discussions over the colossal task at hand.

The leader of the South American clan had sent a simple email with a single word, "Congratulations."

Bethany glanced at her mate by her side. Happiness welled inside her. He gazed back at her with a grin. They were bonded. He could feel the happiness pouring from her as she could feel how proud he was of her. It was incredible. Tears clogged her throat and welled up in her eyes, simply thinking about how much they loved one another.

Yet, she still had a secret to share with him. She planned to tell him tonight, was a bit surprised he hadn't figured it out already because of the bond they shared.

She was pregnant with their child—a new hope for their clan and race growing inside her. A child with ties to two of the four clans and the physical embodiment of their love for one another.

Her prayers for an end to the distrust between the clans and the start of a peaceful coexistence had been answered. An era of change and promise had begun.

A word about the author...

Denise Carbo writes Paranormal Romance, Romantic Suspense, and Contemporary Romance. She is a voracious reader, loves to travel, is fascinated by the supernatural, and enjoys figuring out the culprit of books and movies before the ending is revealed.

She has a bachelor's degree in Business Administration and Marketing and lives in a small, picturesque New England town with her high school sweetheart and their three amazing sons.

Please visit her website—
www.DeniseCarbo.com
—to learn more about her books and to sign up for her newsletter to receive advance information, excerpts, sales, and other fun tidbits about her books and writing life.

CPSIA information can be obtained
at www.ICGtesting.com
Printed in the USA
BVHW080911070819
555303BV00026B/1935/P